IS THIS TRUE ?

by

Rob Etherson

Copyright © 2018 By Rob Etherson

All rights reserved. No part of this publication may be reproduced, distributed, or transmitted in any form or by any means, including photocopying, recording, or other electronic or mechanical methods, without the prior written permission of the publisher, except in the case of brief quotations embodied in critical reviews and certain other noncommercial uses permitted by copyright law. For permission requests, write to the publisher, addressed "Attention: Permissions Coordinator," at the address below.

This is a work of fiction. Names, characters, businesses, places, events, locales, and incidents are either the products of the author's imagination or used in a fictitious manner. Any resemblance to actual persons, living or dead, or actual events is purely coincidental

Publishing Address
PO Box 29
Harltey Street
Monkseaton
Whitley Bay
Tyne and Wear, NE243Nd

E mail:info@lignumrecycling.com

All rights reserved.

ISBN: **9781977085504**

Special thanks to Lisa, Zara
&Tony Tight Pants.

Thanks for believing in me when I couldn't

We're all just looking for who and what we are.

****

Christmas dinner

She should have been excited. On Christmas day, most mothers get excited at the thought of their children and grandchildren arriving to eat dinner and spend the day together. Eileen isn't' most mothers though. She's like some of them, but not all of them. No one really knows how many mothers out there are like her, but it's more than we care to believe. She wasn't excited, happy, positively anxious, or optimistic about the day ahead. Yet, she wasn't sad, ambivalent, negatively anxious or pessimistic about the day ahead either. In fact, she didn't feel much of anything at all. Eileen knew she was the head of the family and everyone should come together to pay their respects, no matter what. Tradition and culture demanded it. In Eileen's mind, feelings about the day were pointless. No sense in wasting energy. After all, she had a lot of hard work ahead and dinner to prepare. In reality, Brent would be skivvying around behind her doing everything else while she cooked. The mopping and cleaning, setting tables and tidying house were all his. He knew what he needed to do without receiving any verbal instructions or encouragement. The idea of actually receiving encouragement from Eileen was one of Brent's many fantasies. A smidgen would do, but it was highly unlikely. Eileen used a sort of coarse body language and contorted facial expressions to let him know what he needed to do next. She would posture and look distortedly in the direction of the area that needed attention, and off he shot like a rabbit avoiding oncoming headlights. If she was ignoring him, he knew he was on the right track. From the outside, it looked as if they worked well together as they cleaned and cooked. They resembled a well-oiled, synchronised team. The nonverbal's between them were subtle. Nearly unnoticeable. Some humans, and most animals, possess an innate ability to work well together. It's an ancient and instinctual practice, which means they can do it without training or previous experience. Two people might never have met in their lives before, yet somehow they can move around a task and perform like seasoned ballet partners. This wasn't the dynamic that was taking place between Eileen and Brent. This was a different thing altogether. Brent was Eileen's life partner. She was glamorous and he wasn't. They looked mismatched. Appearance wise, Brent was a bit short-fattish-nerdy looking with thinning hair and steel-rimmed round spectacles. His skin around his face was too tight and his lips were too plump. Teenagers would call him a computer geek. Probably because he looked and acted like one. Eileen and Brent had been together for fourteen years. As far as everyone knew, he was the only man she had been with since her ex-husband left. She was quick to point this out, but no one knew if it was true or not. Doubt about these dubious facts arose in others who knew Eileen, because her past had a colourful tinge when it came to relationships and sexual exploits. Apart from the obvious incompatibility, their relationship was unusual in lots of other ways. They only spent time together on Tuesday and Thursday evenings, and all-day Saturday until Sunday morning. They took turns to stay over at each other's houses on alternate weekends. Their pattern only changed when they went on holiday. Otherwise, it stayed the same. Everyone around them believed that Eileen was dominant and Brent was subservient to her. In most circumstances, he was. He liked it this way, and she liked it too. It served them both well. The roles they played-out were not contrived in any way. They didn't sit behind closed doors, scheming and planning about how to act in public. They were just like most other couples. They were acting in accordance with who and what they were. She was a certain way and so was he. This was the glue that held them together. It was the same adhesive that holds all relationships together. Theirs was just a particular brand.

Cheryl and Brutus were the first to arrive. Cheryl was Eileen's youngest daughter. She was in her late twenties and a little bit overweight, but she was glamorous and very, very fashion conscious. Brutus was Cheryl's dog. A Chihuahua. Eileen didn't like dogs. This one especially. She had hoped that Cheryl would leave it at home. She should have known better. They were inseparable, those two. Sure enough, Brutus was wearing a Christmas jumper and little reindeer's antlers tied around his head. He didn't look happy about it though. He looked unhappy most of the time and it showed in his disgruntled face. Eileen looked straight at him and smirked. He stared back at her, and she was sure that he was growling under his breath. Cheryl caught wind of the impending duel and intervened by cooing, "C'mon mamas baby boy. Aren't you just the cutest little guy? Come over here Brutus, there's a good lad." Reluctantly, Brutus turned away and trotted back to Cheryl. Eileen's smirk extended across her face a little further, because Brutus's antlers bobbed from side to side in rhythmic time with his tiny feet as he waddled away. To her, the whole scene, and that dog, were pathetic. "I thought Oslo was taking Brutus today, Cheryl?" Eileen asked, in a tone that seemed genuinely inquisitive and caring. Cheryl knew all about her mother's tones and their intentions. This time, both were clearly accusatory and condensing in equal measures. To counteract the jibe, Cheryl parried and complimented Eileen on the cleanliness of the house; the Christmas decorations and the layout of the Christmas table. Eileen was wise to Cheryl's tactics, but she played along anyway. No sense in pushing too hard so early in the day, she thought. Eileen knew where Cheryl's limits lived, and she knew her daughter would push back and storm off in a rage for few days if it went too far. "Thanks, Cheryl. I've been working all day and most of last night to get this house ship-shape. I'm exhausted. I do not know how I will get through the rest of today. I hope the children aren't too noisy when they get here. Natalie and Chad can't control that Jack. They should be firmer with that one. Brent's not much help either. He's watching the football. Again. Or golf, or something." Brent had only switched on the TV three minutes before Cheryl and Brutus arrived. He'd cleaned and polished every corner of the house and he thought he was finished. He had stood still for over nearly five minutes before sitting down and reaching for the remote control. At the same time, he paid close attention to Eileen's movements to make sure that he was on point. She was ignoring him. As far as he knew, this meant everything was good. He was sitting in the big oversized armchair, which backed-on to the open plan kitchen where Cheryl and Eileen were tussling. Cheryl hadn't noticed that he was there. She didn't hear the TV either as the volume was at its lowest setting. Brent was slumped deep into the chair to avoid communicating. He engaged in social pleasantries when he had to, but he didn't like it. He wasn't paying any attention to the sports channel either. He didn't like sports, but everyone left him alone when he watched them. This gave him more time to fantasise. Fantasising was his favourite pastime. He heard Eileen's comments about his laziness and unwillingness to help, yet he didn't attempt to defend himself. He just looked up at Cheryl, all victimised-like, and said, "Hi Cheryl.

Merry Christmas." She returned the seasonal greeting, and then turned to look at her mother in a way that asked why she hadn't extended the same courtesy. To avoid any further disruption so early in the day, Eileen obliged. She wished Cheryl merry Christmas, then leaned in and kissed the air beside her left cheek while making the synonymously middle-to-upper-classed "Mwwwaaa" noise. Cheryl mirrored her mother's gestures and sounds, which gave the act a ritualistic guise. It was over in less than two seconds. The scene appeared excruciatingly superficial and trivial, given that Eileen came from a painfully working-class background, but it held enough power to reset the cement that bound them together in their respective roles as an upwardly-socially-mobile mother and daughter team. For now, they could move on, forget about the previous quibble and re-solidify the illusory nature of their relationship. Unit next time. Then, they would do it all over again.

Natalie, Chad, Joe, Tilly and Jack were next to arrive on the scene. The doorbell rang and Cheryl jumped with excitement at the prospect of seeing her older sister and her niece and two nephews. She rushed to the door to greet them and Brutus sprinted in front of her to get there first. Like all dogs, he knew who was at the door. As Cheryl reached to open the door, Brutus spun around and around with his reindeer ears and Christmas jumper following close behind.

Natalie was Eileen's oldest daughter. She was approaching her fortieth birthday, although she looked ten years younger. She was one of those women who could eat whatever she liked and never gain weight. She hardly ever wore makeup, dressed in tatty jeans and baggy jumpers and walked in bare feet whenever the opportunity presented itself. She had long black hair that always shone; an eternal sun tan and deep green eyes that sparkled like the finest Chinese jade. Somehow, she always appeared relaxed. Her body, underneath the baggy jumpers and jeans, held its posture in a manner that let privileged onlookers know she possessed all of her own personal power. At the same time, her physique looked unperturbed and malleable. She had a bit of a Buddha-ish countenance. In essence, she was effortlessly beautiful. Her temperament and nature matched her loveliness. Eileen knew that Natalie was the re-embodiment of her own mother. When she was younger, Eileen had her mother's looks too. And she still did, even as she passed the mid fifty mark. Otherwise, in comparison to her own mother and Natalie, she was the polar opposite.

Chad, Natalie's husband, was a dumpy little bald guy. He was forty-ish too and looked every part of it. When he was out in public with Natalie, people gawped at them. They were either thinking that Chad was punching away above his weight, or he was loaded and Natalie must be after his money. Chad drank too much, worked too much, talked too much, moved too much, ate too much and sang too much. He moved through life like an effervescent cartoon character. Apart from all of that, he was a genuinely loving and caring human being. His kids idolised and adored him and his friends liked being his friend. In fact, he was utterly likeable in every way.

Joe was Chad and Natalie's oldest child. He was fifteen going on sixteen. His age belied his years. He was a cool kid with a mysterious edge. From an early age, he knew who he was and what he wanted to be. No-one else knew that he knew this, because he kept these things to himself. He also had a habit of asking and answering questions in a very literal fashion. He didn't like ambiguity and wasn't enamoured with adults who treated him like a child. At five years old he began saying things like, "being a child doesn't give you the right to treat me like one." It seemed as if he didn't respect adults and wasn't afraid of them. From early on, he was branded an impudent child with social inadequacies. Schoolteachers and their like tried to encourage Natalie to have him tested on the autistic spectrum. They also suggested that he might even have some Asperger tendencies. Natalie placated those unwanted advisors and never sprung to Joe's defence in their presence. She knew that he didn't intend to be disruptive or disrespectful. It was just the way his mind worked and how he viewed people and things. Personally, she didn't have a problem with his ways, and his dad was fine with them too. Most of the time, they left him alone. They knew that he was destined to find his own way in this life and that he was eager to get at it. Eileen, as always, had plenty to say about Joe. She thought Natalie and Chad were too liberal with him. Often, she would toss in her tuppence-worth by quoting dying philosophies, such as "children need strong guidance" or "they should respect their elders" and "he needs to learn about actions and consequences". Whenever she managed to get Joe on his own, Eileen tried to impose some of these ideas on him. But Joe stood fast and asked her to justify her theories or tell him where they originated. When he did this, Eileen found herself caught between admiring his spirit and quelling the urge to crush him. She never gave any indication that she felt this way, just in case the boy used it against her in the future. Instead, she stared blankly at him until he walked away. Which he did. These encounters were frequent, because Natalie presided over his security whenever Eileen was in the picture. Now, as teenager heading towards adulthood, he was learning to curb his responses when interacting with adults. He hadn't grown tired of them, or afraid of them. He was just beginning to realise that they didn't really want to understand him. And that suited him just fine. If they left him alone, he would leave them alone.

Tilly, Joes younger sister, was the middle child. She was nine years old. A tall, skinny, wispy blonde. Tilly loved spending time and doing things with her mother. She loved her dad just as much. But, she definitely preferred her mother's company. Tilly and Natalie would wile away hours of effortless enjoyment whenever they got the chance. Together, they enjoyed cooking, school homework, cleaning, washing-up, shopping, dressing for a night out, make-up, sewing, knitting, and designing and making their own clothes. Eileen remarked that she thought Natalie was a bit old-fashioned with Tilly. She accused them of being far too "traditionally feminine" for her liking. She even tried telling Natalie that encouraging girls to take part in these types of activities only served to undermine women's rights in a world dominated by men. She attempted to educate Natalie on the subject of feminism, and how strong women throughout the ages had given their lives for such a noble cause. Whenever Eileen came at her in this way, Natalie just smiled and told her mother that everything would be ok and not to worry too much about it. Even as a child, Natalie never seemed fazed by her mother's attempts to impose her will and control over her. This infuriated Eileen. As usual, she never showed it. Eventually, she resigned herself to the idea that Natalie was just too much like her own mother and nothing she ever said or did what change that. From time to time she still tried though, because this is what she did.

Jack, the baby in the brood, was four. Like his mother, he suntanned easily. He had big brown eyes and jet black curly hair to match. The features that he shared with his mother indicated that there must have been some Latin-Mediterranean influence back in their bloodline. Jacks temperament was more in line with his fathers. If he wasn't asleep, he was full of fizz and joyful energy. For a four-year-old, his vocabulary range was impressive. His parents were amazed at some of the words he used. They had no idea where he picked them up or how he knew where they belonged in sentence structures. Every thirty seconds he pointed at things that caught his eye and asked the question, "what's that?" He wasn't asking anyone in particular, he was just asking the question and he expected an answer. If he didn't get one, he just kept asking until he did. Natalie, Chad, Joe or Tilly always took time to reply to his incessant questioning. They didn't mind it. In fact, they encouraged it. If he wasn't talking, he was running, jumping, climbing on furniture or playing with his toys. On occasions, he was allowed to watch cartoons and children's programmes on the TV or i-pad. Not too often though. At his age, his parents were reluctant to use tech devices and digital media as playthings. They knew that in few years these things would become a part of his existence anyway. There was no need to rush him into it. Eileen wasn't fond of Jack's energy and enthusiasm at all. He and it really irritated her. Given free reign, she would quell and stifle both of them. If she got the chance, she would bring him under control by knocking the boisterousness out of him with some correctional slaps and taps. Modern schools of thought were leaning towards criminalising parents who hit their children in any way at all, but Eileen thought this was "poppycock". She believed that punishing children, and meting it out, should be left to parents. In her eyes, government, social workers and woolly-liberal-earth-mother-types were just interfering in busybodies who had nothing better to do with their time. To her, a sharp rap on the backside was a tool that mothers needed to keep children safe and in-line. She didn't have any problems hitting any of her children, she thought. She hardly ever had to, except for her son Kevin, of course. To her, he was an unteachable bad seed. He needed it more than the rest of them. She thought that her grandson Jack wasn't quite as far gone as Kevin, but she was sure he would end up in the same place if his wayward behaviour wasn't curtailed with a firm hand. Once again, Natalie stood quietly and confidently firm between her mother and her children. Eileen held herself quietly and firmly too. But unlike Natalie's confidence, Eileen's stance was laced with contemptuous rage. And as usual, it was almost unnoticeable.

Cheryl opened the front door. Immediately, Brutus and Jack rushed to meet each other. Like all small boys and pet dogs, they were kindred spirits. The fussed roughly over each other and Jack sprinted off into the house with Brutus chasing closely behind. When they reached the conservatory doors at the back of the house, Brutus turned and ran back the other way and Jack became the chaser. Eileen hackles came up behind her smile as the boy and the dog set off on the day's adventures. Cheryl squealed at the site of her sister then flung her arms around her neck and gave her big Christmas welcome, accompanied by three or four loud smacking kisses in quick succession. Natalie returned the compliment with equal measures of love and enthusiasm. Cheryl then gave Chad and Joe a warm hug and wished them the same. She had to go looking for Tilly because she was standing quietly just behind her mother's left leg. Cheryl found her and took a seasonal hug and kiss. Tilly stood sullen and didn't respond. Eileen was making her way towards the entrance of the house to greet everyone and she noticed Tilly's reluctance to return Cheryl's welcome. Without thought, her tone firmed up and she tried to correct Tilly by telling her not to be rude and give her aunty Cheryl a hug. Natalie intervened immediately and told her mother that Tilly would respond in her own way and in her own time, and that everything was just fine the way it was. Natalie's ability to deliver the intervention without offending Eileen, while supporting Tilly, was uncanny. Eileen's emotional defence mechanism had a hair-trigger. The merest slight or insult, either perceived or real, could fire her up into full battle mode. When Natalie disarmed her this time, Eileen felt unusually confused and disoriented. She wanted to launch a counter attack, but she couldn't. Weirdly, she felt complimented and respected. Eileen's delayed reaction gave Natalie the chance to redirect the action; so she moved towards her mother to exchange a festive greeting. Just before they met, Natalie took hold of the outside of her mother's upper arms before she had a chance to raise them. By doing this, she was able to take the lead, much like a dance partner; otherwise, her mother would have pulled her into an overly-tight embrace. Natalie knew fine well that Eileen had a habit of doing this to assert her dominance, and she didn't like it. In a man's world, an overpowering handshake had the same effect. Eileen could only bend her arms up from the elbow and clutch Natalie's in the same way. This allowed them to lean in, kiss each other's cheek and say "Merry Christmas". There was no "Mwwwa" this time. From Eileen's perspective, the whole thing felt awkward and restricted. To Natalie, it was as she intended. Every time they connected physically, which wasn't often, Natalie envisaged gnarled and petrified tree roots. Her mother felt like brittle, cold wood. Chad brought up the rear with Joe following close behind in his footsteps. Both welcomed Eileen in quick flash encounters while Tilly remained her reticent-self. Eileen didn't try to correct Tilly in case Natalie knocked her off-line again. She was reluctant to re-experience those feelings twice in the same day. One by one, Natalie, Chad and Joe wished Brent a Merry Christmas as he sat low in the armchair. When everyone entered the house, Brent didn't stand up to greet them. They excused his lack of social grace because they felt a bit sorry for him, given Eileen's tyrannical ways. All except Tilly that is. She didn't greet Brent because she didn't like him. She could feel his eyes on her when no one else was watching. There was something about those stolen glances that creeped her out. She steered herself well away from him whenever they were in the same place. To everyone else, this transaction went virtually unnoticed. Once or twice in the past, Natalie picked up that something wasn't right quite with Tilly. But Tilly was reluctant to tell her mother about her feelings, just in case she was wrong. She didn't want to cause any fuss or attract attention at the best of times, and it only happened occasionally. There really wasn't that much to it, thought Tilly. Brent limply returned the greetings and turned his head back to his faux TV watching. Before his eyes met the screen, he managed to steal a snapshot of Tilly in her new Christmas outfit. He thought she looked very pretty today. He especially liked her socks. To avoid any further interactions with the babbling voices behind him, he slumped back into position and conjured up one his favourite fantasies while staring blankly into the mash of colours and sounds radiating from the TV in front of him.

Now, all but one of the characters were on stage and the scene was set to play out Christmas day. As expected, Kevin hadn't appeared. Kevin, like Tilly, was the middle sibling between Natalie and Cheryl. He was in his late thirties, and had missed Christmas for the fourth year in a row. No one mentioned his name in case Eileen indulged in one her rants about him.

Like so many other families, this was the only time they came together in this way. On this day and this day only, they gathered to switch on their feelings of comfort and joy, and then set about exchanging gifts before breaking bread. Today, they could deny reality and normality. During the other three hundred and sixty-four days, Eileen was immersed in trivial bickering and everyone's differences with Cheryl hanging on her coattails. Natalie and Chad were aware of their dynamic, and stayed away from it. If they wanted to, they could have stepped out of the circle altogether and taken their children with them. But they didn't. They stayed in the loop because Natalie knew that her sister and absent brother needed her to. Who else could step in to protect them from Eileen when they needed it most? As children growing up, Natalie did her best to nullify the effect of Eileen's abusive and controlling techniques by reassuring her brother and sister whenever she could. Now they were grown adults, yet Cheryl and Kevin were still snared in their mother's clutches. Perhaps one day they might try to break free. If they ever did, she wanted to be there waiting for them.

Eileen took up her position as the head of the family and orchestrated dinner from the top of the table. On more than one occasion, she had to stop herself from reprimanding the kids about their table manners. Natalie's presence inconvenienced her once more. To discharge her frustrations, she turned her attention on Brent by throwing him a series of condescending looks and peculiar gestures. She was telegraphing that there were tables to clear, desserts to serve and dishes to wash. He understood the messages without making too many mistakes. When Brent moved to do as instructed, Tilly caught sight of him in her peripheral vision. For a flickering moment, something alerted her to leave the freedom of childhood forgetfulness until he was out of sight. She hardly recognised the brief warning and returned to fastidiously dissecting her pigs in blankets. Instinctively, Natalie asked her if everything was ok. As usual, Tilly looked up with a quiet soft smile and Natalie felt reassured. Chad made short work of the six beers he brought with him and began putting a dent in Eileen's expensive diner wines on the table. He knew she was watching him and tutting and huffing under breath. He did like a good slurp of red though, so he carried on regardless. He worked hard all year and it was time to enjoy himself. Eileen wasn't going to get in his way. He enjoyed a good drink. When drinking, he was consistent. You could guarantee that the more he drank the happier he became, until it was time to fall asleep. Natalie didn't mind, as long as it didn't happen too often. She knew that if she was concerned about it, and told him, he would stop in a heartbeat. He couldn't bear to think that his behaviour was upsetting her or the kids, and she held the same values.

Joe, being fifteen going on sixteen, wanted to be with his friends. As soon as dinner ended, he left with a quick goodbye, see you later and off out the door. Predictably, Eileen had something to say about that too. This time she tried a different approach, and asked Natalie where he was going on such a special "family" day. Natalie responded in her usual way and told her mother about his age and his needs, and everything would be ok. Eileen felt something unpleasant again, so she used her special code to relay more instructions to Brent.

Cheryl revelled in the opportunity of seeing her sister, so she spent most of the day catching up and chatting with her. She also spent time playing with the two younger kids and sharing mobile phone and social media stories with Joe. She wanted to visit Natalie and her family more often, but she just seemed to be too busy all the time. She was either working, mooching about shopping centres and nightclubs with Oslo, or at her mother's house. In-between all that, she was moving in and out of short-term online fuelled relationships.

Jack fell asleep on the sofa at the beginning of dinner with Brutus tucked up beside him. They awoke just in time to get in on desert and the Facebook Christmas photo shoot. Eileen was carefully choreographing the whole scene to make sure the world saw her as a mother with a respectable, loving, modern family who were happy and had everything they needed in life. The Christmas image wasn't' a one-off event. It was a continuation of the fabricated tale that Eileen, with Cheryl as her key accomplice, had been telling through social media for years. In total, twenty-three photos were taken. Later, when everyone else left, Eileen and Cheryl sifted through them to make sure they were fit for purpose before posting. After that, they used the rest of the evening to obsess over the incoming likes and comments. While they did this, Brent tidied the house. To make his tasks more tolerable, he mumbled and hummed the dialogue and tune of some popular Star Trek scenes. " Dah, dah……dah…..da- dara dah da…….to boldly go where no man has gone before! Ahhh……she's breaking up, I can't hold her Jim………..Live long and prosper captain Make it so number one…!"

Kevin

"Fuck, it's hot". I'm engaged in an activity that most people would call walking. The pace is quick and my steps are short and shifty. My head is up. My darting eyes are scanning left and right in rhythmic time with my feet. I feel and look like an epileptic automaton.

There's a voice in my head. An old friend. Don't ask me why, but it speaks in raspy Scottish accent. And it's saying, *"Never mind about that sonny boyyyyy... one of each...one of each... and we're on our way... we'll be there soon...safe... hurry the fuck up man...but remember...don't fuckin run...no matter what !"*

"Shit, it's really dark tonight". The street lights are out. I'm still skittering along. Same pace. Same face. Same insane game.

"Go on sonny boyyyy...you must go on...go on... nearly there... not long now... one of each... a couple of hundred yards... sanctuary... you and me... but remember... don't fuckin run... no matter what.!

"Bastard, it's muggy." I'm sweating. The heat, the dark and my uncontrollable shoe shuffling are getting out of hand. To make matters worse, there's a transparent skinned insect wrapping barbed tendrils around the base of my spine, and it's threatening to crawl all the way up it. A parasitic infestation is imminent. But this isn't a new sensation. I know exactly what the postman has in his bag before the skanky parcel arrives.

"forget all that shit Sonny Boyyyyyy... keep movin... keep movin... one of each... you and me... a hundred yards... one of

each... get behind the door... fuck 'em all... but remember... don't fukinnnnn runnnnn no matter whatttt !"

"It's far too quiet for my liking". The passage ahead is narrow and seems unfamiliar, although I pass through it every day. I'm hemmed in on both sides by two tight rows of paint-flaked semi-derelict apartments. No gaps or alleys or breaks. Bleak sculptures, topped with crusty, rusted tin-hat roofs. Underfoot, the sun-baked dirt pathway is split down the middle by a meandering stream of infested liquid that vaguely resembles a water-like substance. It's an open sewage drain filled with liquidised shit, diluted with piss and topped with an occasional globule of burst condom and lumps of swollen sanitary towel. Nothing picturesque about this scene at all. Only one way in and one way out. But I'm in hurry, and I'm committed. Half way in and half way out. Quick step, quick step, one two three....

"Bollocks... Sonnyyyy Boyyyyyy... you're paranoid again... how many times do you need to be told... fuck 'em all... fuck 'em all... me and you... one of each... fifty yards... fuck 'em all... it's all good in the hood... just keep on keeping on... won't be long now... you know the drill... one of each... but remember... don't fukin run... don't ever ever fukin run..!

"Yesssss". Nearly there.

"Fuck... shit..., who's this cunt?" An emaciated figure is skulking in a recessed doorway. He's up ahead on the left, just ten yards away from my exit out of this effluent-riddled gauntlet. He's failing miserably at trying not to look like the dodgiest prick on the planet. Even in this hot, dark and sticky silence, it's clear that his only redeeming feature is his untamed Afro. The fucker. It looks like someone's pulled an electrocuted badger's arse over his dome and tied its legs under his ears.

"Fuckety fuck fuck".

Righteee-oooo Sonny Boyyyyyy... listen to me... listen up... I'm taking the helm... this ship's mine... no ifs... no buts... pay close a-fuckin-ttention. First thing to do is... develop your good old "fuck-this-cunt" attitude... fuck 'im and his pals... fuck 'im and his family... fuck 'im and everybody else that knows 'im............ just like they say on a radio-show phone-ins...

Theeee most important thing to remember..., apart from don't fukin' run of course... is one of each... nobody... but nobody...ever... ever... gets near one of each... understood kemomsabi?... No cunt... Got it?

"Got it".

As sure as shit dipped in sherbet, Afro-boy steps out of his hidey hole as I get up close. The dirt path excuse-for-a-street is only about six or seven-foot-wide, so I can't pirouette and employ my patented body swerve on the skinny bastard. And anyway, just as I'm considering my options his mate mysteriously appears just behind me. Judging by his appearance, he must have been hiding inside one of the used condoms that floated past a few moments earlier. A proper spunk-ridden slime-ball if ever I saw one. He's got an Afro and complexion to match his badger-bonneted mate up front. They have about three teeth between them and big popping eyes that make them both look as if they've just been swiftly evicted from a haunted cuckoo clock.

"I'm in trouble here"

Nonsense Sonnnyyy Boyyyy! Been here before... nothing new here... seen it... done it... heard it...t-shirt...got it...this pair o' jakey bastards don't know what they're in for... me-n-you... one of each... all for us... none for them... get ready... get greedy... you ready?

Ready! – "What do you two shite hawks want" I dryly choke. "Give", they countered, in some broken glassed dialect that utilises just about all of this godforsaken country's eleven different languages. "We've followed from your flat and back. So give", I'm ordered. As soon as number one assailant glanced over my left shoulder to Trojan Johnny behind me, I smashed my forehead directly into the space that once housed his missing gnashers. When forehead bone met toothless gum, his legs deserted him and he headed directly for the floor. His dodgy accent hadn't improved much with all the blood and spit he was swallowing, but I'm sure he was trying to convey some sort of verbal objection. I thought my timing was perfect as I swung my left leg to the right and sprung daintily into my aforementioned patented pirouette. I intended to show semen-features a high class swerve-of-the-body, but no such luck. He threw a right hook from behind and it that blasted me just under my right ear. Dry-gulched me, as they say in spaghetti westerns. He was a skinny runt, so it didn't have much impact and I was out of the blocks like a seasoned one hundred metre sprinter. I shot across the last few yards to my front door. Turned the handle. Dived in. Slammed it shut. Bolted. "Phewf, close one."

Sonnnyyy Boyyyy! Sonnnyyy Boyyyy! Well done... Well done... told you didn't I... I was right again, wasn't I... eh... eh... eh. Can't deny it... no one can... one of each... run like fuck... best policy... stick by me... good man... good man... Right, stop fuckin' about and let's get on with it.

"Right, let's get on with it" I muttered to myself. It's a strange phenomenon. When I'm back in the pad with the door shut and one of each in hand, the imminent spine crawling teem subsides. Bizarrely, it is replaced by thoughts and scents of daisies, daffodils and frolicking through the meadows on a warm spring afternoon. Bees buzz and cows moo and all that, and all that. For those that don't know it, one of each equals one white and one brown; one bag of white crack cocaine and one bag of golden brown heroin. One for me, and one for me. None for you two bandits. So boo-fukin-hoo-hoo you pair of bubble featured bastards. Cunts.

"You said it Sonny Boy, my boy. Now... Hurry up!"

"Right, let's get on with it," I screamed at myself and the empty flat. "Stop fuckin', fuckin' about." I get to it, and start to prepare the ammonia-tainted crack. My neck is throbbing like fuck. I rub it with the palm of my hand, find a small smear of blood, and stare at it for a few seconds. I wonder if the blood belongs to someone or something else. That jiz-encrusted ambushing bandit must've packed more of a punch than I thought. He must've caught me with a stinky fingernail or something. I hope he didn't have any diseases.

Rocking up time! Ever so gently, I rest the little crystallised white rock of crack cocaine into its little glass pipe and sit it on its little circular gauze mesh with lots of little cigarette ash. The cigarette ash stops the goodies from falling through the gauze. The crack always gets it first. That's the procedure. That's the process. Anyone who knows everyone knows that. The heroin gets done afterwards. Only because it counteracts the sheer panic that follows the pathetically quick but powerful rush from the crack. Hitting the crack on its own, without the brown to follow up, is a psychological and emotional disaster zone. I know, because I've done it. Loads of times. Even when I knew what the consequences were going to be. No one knows exactly why I keep making the same mistake. Especially me. So the pipe is loaded and ready to fire. But not quite yet. There's a wee bit more work to be done laddie...

Sonnnyyy Boyyyy! Pleeeeease... Pleeeeease... Pleeeeease... c'mon... hurry up.

Next, prepare the heroin. Cook it up. One never tries to prepare the heroin on a crack come-down, you know. Disaster may ensue at the most inappropriate point in time. Like spilling it, for example. Done that a few times before as well. And each time my screams sounded like a donkey getting a hot baked potato shoved up its arse. I push on with the task in hand and relieve my trusty bent spoon from the darkness of the small worn leather pouch it occupies; alongside its cousins Henry the hypodermic syringe and its brother Tommy the tourniquet. I bought the bent spoon from a car boot sale in Bristol, where the salesman told me it was once used as a prop on a Uri Geller TV show back in the 70's or 80's. I cant remember when. I was blitzed at the time and gave him twelve pounds fifty for it. Lying bastard. It's a good spoon though. Been all over the world it has. I even thought of naming it once or twice, but then I thought that people might think I was a bit weird. So, I didn't bother. If it did have a name, I would call it Bernie. Bent Bernie. Bent Bernie, Tony Tourniquet, and Hypodermic Henry. Porno names if ever I heard them.

"Fuuuuckkkinnnn Hellllllll Sonny Boy - Get on with it, you absolute muppet"

"OK, ok, ok." Spoon, needle, tourniquet, water, lighter, filter, citric acid and heroin. Bish, bash, bosh. All done and sorted. Ready to go when the time comes. And the time is coming. Soon. The process of "cooking up" looks exactly like the scene in Pulp fiction with John Travolta. That was as real as I've ever seen it.

Crack Action.

Click, spark, whoosh goes the cheap disposable lighter. Sook, sook, sooooook goes the inhale and RAAASSSSP RAAAATTTLE CRAKLE goes the damaged alveoli as they fight for survival when the crack fumes soar into my lungs. Alveoli are delicate membranes that live in the lungs. They're used in the oxygen exchange process. Crack cocaine destroys them, and everything else in the respiratory system. Hence the term, "the man died of Crack Lung". Us drug addicts are one of the world's foremost authorities on our chosen subject. Drugs, and what they do for you. Especially illegal ones. It stands to reason. We seek them out and eat, smoke, inject and ingest them any way we can. Twenty-four hours a day, all the year round. We know all about their countries of origin, their component constitutions, and their taste and smell. We specialise in bastardising them for maximum effect and profit. Most of all, we know all the ways and means to get them, and all the ways and mean to get more. At any cost and at everyone else's expense, of course. If you want to know anything about drugs and what they do for you, ask a junkie. Or you could always go see your doctor, I suppose. Or a pharmacist, even.

Back to the crack action.

Whizz, bang wheeeeeeee goes the crack cocaine, as it floods my brain with ridiculously excessive amounts of dopamine and delivers a very short but extremely potent boost to the body's central nervous and reward system. Some say that buzz is so potent, that it's equivalent to five simultaneous orgasms. I'm not sure how they tested that suspect theory, but I do hope they filmed it and put it on You Tube.

To accompany the manic buzz-rush, my heart rate spikes and my blood pressure immediately follows suit. My temple pounds and the veins in my forehead protrude like fattened earthworms crisscrossing just below the surface in a plate of old cold custard. The custard analogy is accurate because I've contracted hepatitis C and my liver is packing up. I'm "Homer-Simpson yellow.

BOOOOOOM! The artery in my neck explodes and projectile blood erupts across the room from the small wound inflicted by Jizzy-Jeff ten minutes earlier. It turns out, he stabbed me with a weapon of choice used by street muggers in this part of the world; a crude hand-fashioned metal spike that protrudes from a carved wooden handle, much like a carpenter's bradawl. The ideology behind these types of weapon is similar to some those used by prison inmates across the globe when they have quibbling tiffs with each other. A few quick blows delivered to a non-lethal area (not the neck) will wound and put the victim into shock and stop him in his tracks. So, the stabber won't end up in court on a murder charge, but he gets his point across. In a way, it's calculated risk . Either way, the stabee loses every time.

Now, I'm in a bit of a panic pickle. Firstly, my immediate

concern is the torrent of blood spurting from neck. So, I plug the gap with lots of pressure and my index finger. It works. Result. Secondly, I'm in the throes of crashing crack come-down, which in itself measures nine-point-five on the Richter scale. I need to inject the heroin into my femoral vein, quick style. And thirdly, I only have one hand available to do it, because I'm using the other in the fashion of a little Dutch boy who's trying to save his village.

Snap to the encyclopaedic nature of a drug addict's knowledge around all things druggy worldly and, he'll inform you that the Femoral vein runs up the inside of the groin and is accompanied by the Femoral artery. It's the go-to vein for us injecting addicts when all other veins have collapsed from years of stabbing and jabbing needles into them. We have even been known to outperform experienced medics when attempting to locate and draw blood from ourselves when hospitalised. The damage and infections that result from injecting in these areas is the most common factor attributed to the loss of limbs. Even then, it's not uncommon for us to start injecting in the other leg and treating the loss as a mere flesh wound. Ha ha, we chunter, as we wheel ourselves back to our favourite drug dealer.

"Right Sonny Boy... don't run... but hurry up... I've got a plan for us... first things first... all you need to do is........

The heroin loaded syringe is sitting on a small square table at the other end of the room. I stagger across and stare at it. The crack come-down is getting worse and my threefold panic-stricken mania is doubling by the second. With the deftness and dexterity of a one-handed pirate, I whip off my leather belt and fashion a buckled noose. I drop my jeans and tattered baggy Y-fronts and feel for the familiar pulse in my groin with my free mitt. I find the vein and stare back at the syringe. I repeat this action about ten times per second for another two or three minutes. Then I grab the looped belt, sling it over my head and around my neck and tighten it around the wounded area with my finger still in place. With timing and sleight of hand that would put a Swiss watchmaking pickpocket to shame, I pull my finger away and tug the belt shut in a flash. I wait for a second to see if the bleeding stays stopped. Not quite. But enough for me to snatch up the syringe, relocate the vein in my groin and shoot the shit in. It's in, and one of the most powerful analgesics on the planet flushes through my bloodstream. Again, like the crack, but in reverse, it stimulates the release of the dopamine, causing the most wonderful sensation of wellbeing and exquisite pleasure. With that, my brain and body relaxes. My heart beat slows and my blood pressure drops. But I can't fucking breath because I've just about hung myself with the belt. I loosen it a little and allow myself the privilege of airflow. I keep the belt where it is, just in case I'm required to re-employ the medieval band aid. The blood stays stopped as planned. From the other side of the room, lying on the table with the rest of the paraphernalia, Tony the Tourniquet looks as if he's feeling bit redundant. Out loud, to myself, in Batman's voice, I sound the charge "to the hospital". Trouble is, I'm living in a rat infested shit pit in the middle of a ghetto. Buses don't exist and taxis drivers wouldn't dare come anywhere near the place. Police and priests give it wide berth to. On top of all that, I don't have a phone or any money. The nearest medical help is at least two miles away, so I need to hoof through outlaw outback to get there. This time, I launch into my best thespian impersonation and give it some Shakespearean lilt, "Once more unto the breach, dear friends, once more; Or close the wall up with our English dead." Crack and heroin are good for that sort of role play. With carefree abandon, I can be anyone I like.

On the way back to the flat from my dealers, my gait and stride pattern had certain piquancy. On the trudge back out to find medical help, whilst inebriated with a big dose of Afghan's and Columbia's primary exports, my cadence was filled with meaning and purpose. Occasionally, it was interrupted by a pit stop for a good old gouch. A gouch is what commonly takes place when one is fucked on heroin. No matter where I am or what I'm doing, I come all over all fuzzy and warm and involuntarily fall into a type of lucid dreaming half-sleep affair. It's similar to narcolepsy, although narcolepsy doesn't cost as much. Then all of a sudden, I'm up and off again. And I don't even remember breaking stride. Apparently. The term gouch is derived from Mexican cowboys, known as Gauchos, who were often seen sleeping, sitting up, under their sombreros and ponchos. Dodgy folklore at best.

I'm pounding along the hardened dirt with a belt hanging around my neck. I pull on its tail occasionally and hold it, to make sure the blood stays at home. After an hour, I'm clear of mugger's jungle. I'm walking on tarmac road as a car rolls slowly past. There's a young kid in the rear passenger seat pressing his face against the window, and he stares straight at me for a few seconds. I imagine the conversation he's having with his parents as they disappear over a crest. "Daddy, that man was wearing a dog leash and he's taking himself for a walk."

It's about one o'clock in the morning and the lights of a semi-civilised society are getting closer. The drugs are wearing thin and the dried blood is feeling thick. I've managed to keep it at bay for now, but the threat of another rupture keeps the fear level up. I know that I need to get the wound treated as soon as possible.

When I eventually get there, the medical emergency room is chocked full. Its jam packed with every imaginable victim and every imaginable accident and incident. People have been shot, stabbed, robbed and shagged; battered, hammered, chopped and choked; broken, bent, stunned and burned; and the queue for treatment is a mile long. At a glance, it's obvious that waiting-wounded are the poorest of the poor and the medical centre don't look that far behind them.

I'm heading towards heroin withdrawal again, so the base of my spine spasms and bucks like fettered bees in burning hive. I look like a boiled turd, sporting a pasty buttercup complexion, a belt for a necktie and blood caked rags. I look around the medical centre and there's human debris all over the dance floor. I fit right in.

I'm scouring the horizon, trying to attract the attention of a rough-shod medic as he passes by. He's in a hurry. Bodies on trolleys are dying. He doesn't even glance in my direction. For the second time tonight, but on a much more serious note, I say to myself "I'm in fuckin' trouble here."

"Told you Sonny Boy... but no, no, no, no, no... as per usual... didn't listen... never do... can't say I didn't say so... I said RUN ya cunt... imagine letting a couple of wino shit balls get the better of you and stab you in the neck with an old darning needle... you absolooooooooooooooot tit... what a wank job of

an arsehole you are.

Right Sonnyyyyyyyy Boyyyyyyyyyyyy... that wound looks like its healed up to me... we've got business to attend to... money to get... gear to be got... the postman's coming up the path... and we both know what in his sack... let's get to fuckeroony…………sharpish like!

My neck bumps and pulses as my blood pressure rises and I hit first stages of withdrawal. The thumpity thump in my neck gets 's louder. Booom goes that artery again and it explodes once more. I hear an ear-piercing shriek and wonder if the gusher has splattered the wounded patient sitting next to me. Just before I pass out, I realise that the ear piercing shrill originated from just below my nose. I remember my younger years and I'm back in in the UK playing football in the street, using jumpers and jackets as goalposts. I cry out "I hate fucking football" and wonder how I ever ended up in the bum-hole slums of South Africa with a hole in my neck. I think of my mother, Eileen, and how I miss her. Blackness.

Brutus

What's that smell?

Ok, ok. So, I'm a Chihuahua. Who gives a shit. Not me. No way. No doubt about it! What I don't have in size, I make up for in stature, pure bottle, dazzling charisma and massively oversized bollocks. When her gay best friend, Oslo, first seen them, he put on his best teenage girl's voice and with all the minceyness he could muster, he bleated "eeeeehhh... Cheza... look at his nads. They're heeyoooge. They look like a couple of golf balls swinging about in a Tesco's carrier bag". Oslo's bleat is hard to hear.

I'm cute to look at. Yeah. Maybe. But mark my words because I'm proper narky. Stands to reason. You would be as mumpy as me, if you were treated like a fashion accessory and paraded around all day in a ridiculously overpriced handbag while being forced to wear horrendously multi-colored woolly outfits and matching sunglasses in seventy-five-degree heat. Her surrogate child, she calls me. If a child had the misfortune of ending up with this balloon as its mother, then the little thing would be doomed to suffer the same fate as most of its peers. No doubt, the kid would be stuffed in a stroller and pushed down the high street, while daft-arse follows behind with her head stuck in a mobile phone because someone farted on Facebook and indirectly blamed one of her imaginary three-hundred-and-seventeen friends for the smell. Feigning disgust with a series of low lipped ssssss sounds and tut-tut-tuts, she'd be double-thumbing some opinionated response about the varying degrees of fart sounds and smells. Meanwhile, the child with the buggy strapped to its back would meander into on-coming

IS THIS TRUE ?

traffic and she'd hardly notice until it was too late.

The thought of this is leaving me feeling grateful for the safety and comfort of this gaudy handbag. I know I'm safe in here because she places an exorbitantly high value on the bag. She wouldn't dream of losing touch with it for a nanosecond. Corporate marketing strategies that hypnotise their victims into believing that self-worth costs money and the more you spend the more you get took root in the subconscious of this wanna-be-diva a long time ago. These values are deeply embedded in her, and they're here to stay. So is the handbag. But she doesn't know that know that its sparkle will fade in time, or that she'll forget all about it when the next must-have trinket flashes across one of her screens. Until then, she'll treasure it.

know that

Anyhow, enough of that. Where was I. Oh yeah. Right. Woolly outfits and seventy-degree heat. So here's me, saddled in a handbag with a chronically self-obsessed thirty-something female who compares herself to the ex-Mrs Cole just because she's got the same first name. She'll detach from her idol when her fame wanes and she moves back towards obscurity. No sense in idolising a has-been. I wonder if famous people remember what obscurity was like? After all, that's where they all come from. If the Americans are to be believed, which apparently they're not, an awful lot of famous people suffer as their popularity and appeal dissipates into the ether. When this happens, some put a gun in their mouth, and some of them even pull the trigger. It doesn't make sense. When famous people start out in life, like most other humans, the only people who really cared whether they lived or died was their family members and maybe a few good friends. Then they get famous. After that, they pass through their fame-life and pop out at the other end. When they return to join all the other people who live normal everyday existences, some are lucky enough to have a few people left in their life who would shed a tear for their pain. A lot of them fall apart anyway. Stranger still, millions of others yearn for fame and do everything they can to get it. Eventually they realise it was a pipe-dream and they've fallen way short of the mark. So, they fall apart too. I'm glad that I'm a dog.

Cheryl, my owner, is a classic case. She signed up as a fully-fledged club member in the wanna-be club a long time ago. She's not famous yet, but she has added some volume to the teeming hordes of other limelight junkies. Put them under a spotlight or in front of a TV camera, and they go off like a starving vampire feasting on virgin's blood. Cheryl remains eternally optimistic in the face of overwhelming odds. She's convinced, that with her glowing presence she'll command the X-Factor stage at some point in the very near future. The fact that she can't sing, dance or teach sheepdogs to do tricks is nothing but a mere inconvenience to her. I've heard her talking to Oslo on more than one occasion about how her amazing good looks, fabulous physique and her magnetic charm will win the judges over in spite of her dire lack of talent. During these outbursts, Cheryl and Oslo gee each other along like frolicsome school kids. I know I can be a tad melodramatic, and I have a tendency to over-egg the custard from time to time, but there's no other way to describe the excruciatingly painful spasms that leave me barfing and retching when I listen to this pair of headbangers as they launch themselves into a full-blown conversation. If I had fingers, I'd stick them in my ears. Soul crushing doesn't cut the mustard. Listen to me and my analogies eh! All mustard and custard and other types of turd.

If those two are not talking to each other, then they're usually talking about each other and how fabulous they are. Surprisingly, they don't bitch-n-backstab each other. I don't think the realise it, though. If they did, it would have them "ooohhing" and "ahhhhing" in metronomic time. "Ooooooh Oslo!" she would shriek. Then, in a squeaky-toy-toned voice that elongates the first three words and over-emphasises every syllable, she'd say something like, "Yooooou, arrrrre, notttttt going to believe this. Ohhh... Mmmmm... Geeee! I was reading NOW magazine this morning and I came across this article, which obviously is so so true. It said that women and their male GBF's don't bitch behind each other's backs. It says that they are totally totally loyal. That's Wuuuuuunnn... Hunnnnddred... Perrrr... Centtt... me and you Oslo. Wunnnnnn... Hunnndred! With hands on hips, eyes at the sky and a wide open-mouthed gawp, Oslo would join in enthusiastically. Using the same exaggerated speech patterns, he's squeal, "Ooooooooh... I... knowwwwwah. I read it too, and just knew it was me and you. It's just so so us. Ohhhhhh... Mmmmmmm ... Geeeee, I could hardly believe it. I know for an absolute fact, without any doubt, that it's so so troooooooo!" Cheryl's the dominant one of these two, so she always takes the lead and has the last word during all of their little tête-à-têtes. If her guard fell and a hint of humility began bubbling to the surface, she would be forced into allowing Olso, or anyone else for that matter, think or feel that they might be equal in some way. Then, the cracks would start to appear in the foundations that underpin her humongous sense of entitlement. An enduring quality that her mother spent years training her to perfect; and one that she shares with the rest of her painted peers. So, she's not going to let that happen now. Is she? Nooooo... Fuckinggggg...

Waaaayyyah! So off she would trot and attempt to convince Oslo that she knows why it's an absolute fact, without any doubt whatsoever, that women and their GBF's don't bitch-n-backstab. "I'm telling you Oslo, it's so so simple to understand. Everyone knows that. It's all about sex. The thing is, you see, is that women and their GBF's, like me and you, don't want to have sex with each other or with anyone else that either of them wants to have sex with either. Simple". In time-honoured fashion, Oslo would obediently and repeatedly nod his pea-sized head while displaying all the traits of a subservient pet pooch while Cheryl prattled on. This would let "Cheza" (the name she allows Oslo, and absolutely one else, to use) know that he thought she was so so correct, and he just absolutely so so agreed with everything she was saying. Really, he was just bewildered. But somewhere in the back of his mind, he would hear a faint voice that sounded just like his. It would say, "Bollocks Cheza. The only reason we don't assassinate each other's character, just like the majority of the narrow-minded soul suckers that we knock about with, is because we co-sign each other's bullshit in a parody of a relationship that is built on compliance. In reality, you're a bit of a bully and I'm a bit of coward. Sticking together just helps us to hide from ourselves, the world and all the people in it. These thoughts would be blasphemous. They would never see the light of day. He would feel that there was some truth to them though. Eighteen months earlier during a conversation about the "chem-sex" scene in the gay community, Cheza was force-feeding Oslo with her profound and in-depth knowledge on the subject. She was twittering on about how she knew why so many gay men were doing it and suffering because of it. Involuntarily Oslo sat titling his head to the side, mimicking an inquisitive Labrador pup looking for runaway rolls of Andrex. At the same time, he pulled a strange face that suggested he had a counter-argument in response to Cheza's theory. Big mistake. Instantly, she picked up the slightest whiff of a hint that he was thinking about disagreeing with her. Worse still, he looked as if he was actually going to put a voice to those ungodly thoughts. Ka-Booooomm. Chez's exaggerated sense of entitlement went nuclear. Poor Oslo was blown off his feet. It wasn't by the look of utter disgust that Cheza bestowed upon him. The damage came from the glowering intensity in the putrid rage that she sent his way, and the fact that she made very little effort to hide it. He really nearly shit. He really, really, did. He hadn't felt anything as intense as this since he made the stupid mistake of declaring his sexual preferences to his parents when he was thirteen years old. His father's reactions hurt most on that day. He didn't want to, but his feelings about his sexuality overpowered him. They forced him into facing his darkest fears and telling his truth to those that were supposed to love him most.

Norman, Oslo's dad, was one of those Neanderthal type chaps who walks, talks and looks like a bigoted racist with Tourette's syndrome. Neanderthal Norm. That should have been his nickname down at the local working men's club. You only had to see or hear the man dragging himself along the pavement to predict what his response would have been. What was Oslo hoping for? Whatever it was, his mother didn't offer him any of it either. He didn't really blame her though. He knew what she lived with, and what she would face if she did say or do anything to support him. . Why his mother stayed with that man was anyone's guess. Some say women who stay with abusive men are trapped victims. Others say, that they stay because of the benefits. Whenever he tried to understand it, he drew a blank and fell into utter confusion. From that day, Oslo did everything he could to avoid re-feeling his parent's wrath. The mere idea of arousing Cheryl's scorn warned him of the imminent threat. Instinctively he dismissed his intuition and opinion on the "chem-sex" scene, even although he was an avid participant in it every weekend and on the occasional weekday. And like so many times before, he tried hard to swallow as he choked on his own words. And like so many times before, he felt exposed and tried to cover it up. This time, to throw Cheryl off balance and off the scent, he pranced across the room and put on his best Liza Minnelli stage show impersonation. Then, he pea-headedly nodded and sang his way out of trouble by changing the subject to shopping for Cheryl's next life-changing purchase. They'd danced this dance many times before, so Cheryl backed up and forced some laughter at Oslo's antics to let him off the hook. Normal service resumed. Chez and Oslo's parents were similar in many ways.

I'm glad I'm a dog! Although, don't associate me with those toilet roll chasing mutts. More fame-seeking sell-outs. As for Oslo and his chem-sex antics, I can't judge. I'll bang anything and join any gang to do it. Given the chance, I'll bang female dogs, male dogs, and male or female human legs. I'll even bang cuddly toys and fresh air. The fresh air thing is when it looks as if I'm humping something but there's nothing underneath me. I need to reign it in from time to time. Cheryl says if she finds any more dog spunk in her furry slippers then she's taking me to the vets to get my stones chopped off and replaced by prosthetic ones. Who came up with that idea? Prosthetic mutt nuts? What's the point of that? Probably that Spanish midget, Cesar Millan. Or is he Mexican? Yeah, he's Mexican. All chooshing and shooshing and finger-clicking and convincing people that the "aesthetic influence of prosthetic balls will negate the loss of the dog's self-esteem. Being able to still see and lick his beans will fool the dog into believing he still has them." Yeah. Right, Caesar. Don't see Gulf War veterans getting picked first for a three-legged race just because of their increased self-esteem due to a rubber leg, do we? No!

Oslo changed the subject again, just to make doubly sure that they didn't revisit the "chem-sex" scenario. Oslo asked Cheryl about her brother Kevin, and if she or anyone else had heard from him yet. He'd been missing for four years and no-one knew where he was. Even the police. And they knew him well. Her response was always the same whenever Kevin's name was in the frame. "Tuttt Tshhhhh Hfffff Hhhimmmm!" When she uttered these noises, she unknowingly took on her mother's persona. Her body shape moved, her facial expressions transformed and her stance, step and hand gestures mimicked her mother's exactly. She also did that thing that her mother does when she means business. She elongated the first and last letters in the first four words of her sentence, with a long pause in between each word. Eileen specialised in this technique and had it down to a fine art. She did it to let unfortunate recipients know that she carried some clout; that she was someone with authority. Most of all, the tactic said she was a person of power and stature. If you were observant enough and knew both of them well enough, Cheryl's transformation looked mystical. Magic even. But it wasn't.

Cheryl cloned her mother and replied to Oslo's question by saying, "Ddon'ttt   ttalkkk ttoooo mmeee about that MANNNN. He's a weak and pathetic junkie. He's trouble, and always will be. All he's ever done is upset all of the family. My Dad doesn't speak to anyone in the family because of him. My poor poor mother got divorced because of him, and she nearly had a nervous breakdown too. My gran died because of everything he did. She just couldn't take it anymore. He's lied, cheated and stole everything from everybody and never did anything to help anyone. He's a waste of time. Always has been, always will be. A pure no-hoper. End of. With a bit of luck, we'll never see him again. Good riddance to bad rubbish. Junkie." She finished off with a "Tuttt Tshhhhh Hfffff, " just the way her mother does.

For the second time in as many minutes, Oslo started falling inwards,. He had tried to dodge a bullet and ended up in her cross hairs - again. He really nearly shit. He really did. Taking evasive for the third time, he asked how her mother was. Especially since her "little incident" the other day. The little incident in question was a hairdo disaster. Her mother had been to the hairdressers and asked for an inch off the length and for her roots to be touched up. It did not go as planned. The hairdresser took off half an inch too much and the hair dye didn't match with her ridiculously high and unachievable expectations. She places high and unachievable expectations on everyone and everything. She has standards to maintain, you know! She wouldn't allow anyone to think less of her. It was a minor event that took place just above her eyebrows and just under her hat that day, but she could've fooled you into believing that it was cataclysmic world tragedy on the same scale as the Japanese Tsunami back in 2011. She was wearing a hat. She said that "…the shame of it was just too much for her." Using her infamous start-up routine, while throwing in a few fake sobs, she cackled, "Hhhhhoowww aaammmm I supposed to go outside in this dreadful condition?" Oh the fucking woe of it!

Eileen doesn't like me. And that's just the way I like it. And that's just the way it's gonna stay. She tries to give me the old "glad eye" every time she sees me. But she knows not to get too close. I stare the bag out just for the crack. Left her with a few broken false fingernails last year when she tried to poke me in the ribs when Cheryl wasn't looking. Big mistake, Eileen. Not only did she lose a few manicured digit-ends, but Cheryl cottoned-on to the attempted rib-jab and went berserk with her. Instantaneously, Eileen had to muster all of her Voodoo powers and conjure up some intense feelings of guilt in Cheryl to get her back where she needed her. So, she bobbed and sobbed and brought Cheryl's dad into the fray by lying through her cosmetic implants about her dad's dog, Rusty. All about how he had treated the dog better than her. And that's why she didn't like dogs. And that's why she didn't like me that much. And I had tried to bite her first when Cheryl's back was turned. And she was just retaliating. Then, she turned the bobbing and sobbing up full-tilt, and ragdoll flopped into Cheryl's arms. She wailed at being all alone most of the week because Brent would only visit She didn't know what she would do without Cheryl. She did and said all of this in one exhale, without a break. And she managed to check in the mirror behind Chery's back to make sure that she hadn't smeared her mascara. After the reflection checking, she narrowed her eyelids into little slits and sneered at me as I watched the whole show from my perch on the sofa. I stiffened my front legs in defiance and gave her a good teeth-showing. I psycho-eyed the bag. She flinched and her slanted eyes widened with doubt and surprise, because she could see and feel that I was a serious contender. She knew I would go all-in if it came to the crunch. Bullies do that when they meet their match. I'll bide my time with this cunt. Harbouring grudges is one of my strong points.

Oslo must have had his diamante-encrusted shovel with him, because the hole he was digging for himself just got bigger and bigger, and it was about to cave in on him. Cheryl was on form.

What is that smell?

Kevin

Sonny boy... sonny boy...what the fuck are you doing?... you and me... we both know that this is a baaaadddd ideeea man! ....Don't do it......................There's gear to be got back in the valley..........back in the land of the free............... the home of the brave............ just because a couple of desperados nicked your neck and it bled for a wee bit............ doesn't mean you need to get all shitty pants about and it and bolt out of dodge at the first sign of a little fracas man...............what are thinking of... this is a baaaaddd ideeea man!............. you know it is.............c'mon........... don't do this sonny boy... me 'n you............ we can take these cunts and run that town ... please sonny boy... don't...

I'm engaged in an activity that most people would call waiting. I'm not good at it. Can't say that I've had much practice. Who would ever want to be good at that anyway? Waste of fucking time, if you're asking me. Why wait, when you could be doing something more interesting instead. No point in facing yourself and your reality now, is there? That's what I always say. That reminds me of that TV show from back in the 80's, or something. Can't quite remember. It was called..., wait for it... "Why Don't You Go Switch off Your Television Set and Go and Do Something Less Boring Instead?" They abbreviated that mouthful, wrote a dodgy theme tune to go with it, and called it "Why don't You?" I was about eight or nine years old and I thought that it must have been the most self-defeating idea ever. It didn't make any sense. They designed a TV programme for kids to encourage them to watch less TV, as it was allegedly rotting their brains. They said the same about kids and their brains and their moral fibre with the invention of rock and roll back in the 50's, and they're saying the same thing about kids and computers and mobile phones today. The thing is, the show was a hit and ran for years. Kids couldn't get enough of it, so they kept the TV switched on, and they still love rock and roll today, and they're not going to give up their mobile phones or laptops any day soon. So leave them alone you bunch of fuckers. That's what I always say. I'm sure that's where I first saw that spoon-bending twat Uri Geller. Four fucking hour delay. And all I can do is wait, wait, wait. The hospital staff phoned my family back in the UK when I was out for the count. They encouraged them to get me a plane ticket to get me out of this shit hole as soon as possible, by scaring them into believing that I wouldn't survive much longer if they didn't. A social-worker-type sorted the gig out. So here I am. Waiting.

The hospital gave me a big injectable dose of a heroin substitute just before discharging me. They topped me up with a few more doses in tablet form for the plane ride home, just to make sure that I didn't spasm into a mid-flight heroin withdrawal and puke all up the centre aisle. A detoxification pack, they called it. I guess they thought I might frighten the more deserving cash-paying customers. Detoxification pack? I was unconscious in hospital for thirty hours and discharged after fifty. I don't think they realise that a decent detox takes at least a week or two to complete, and that's only if there are no other drugs in the fray apart from heroin. I should know. I've hitched a lift on that bone-shaking ride on more than a few occasions. In truth, a good drug habit, or any other addiction, is just one long movement to and from withdrawal symptoms anyway. The first few months is exciting and good fun, and all that. But when the holiday period ends, it's all aboard for an up and down rodeo ride to nowhere, with a liberal dose of fucking over as many people as possible on the way. Especially the ones that need you.

As for the know-it-all fuckers who planned my in-flight fiesta back to Britain were concerned, they'd written up a chemical menu that didn't take into account all of my dietary requirements. A more polite person would say said that they'd miscalculated by a tad, and under-prescribed by a little bit more than they really should have. Someone like me would say something more eloquent. A couple of hundred milligrams of heroin substitute tablets wouldn't blow the froth of my cappuccino. For the past seventeen years, I've been propping up and propelling my mind, body, and mortal-self with a mixture of some of the most powerful illicit and non-illicit substances known to man, and the residual impact of this self-inflicted experiment started kicking in when I woke up from my stab-wound-induced slumber this morning. All manner of scientists, doctors, and theologians have postulated on the physical, emotional, and psychological symptoms of drug-induced withdrawal, and they've written a thousand books on the subject to boot. But very few have had the balls to go and test their theories in the field. The ones that did found out that it's not the kind of experience that can be explained with the written word, and the ones that made it back to the land of the living were too fucked up by the end of their expedition to be bothered with such trivialities anyway. Trainspotting No1 did a decent job of demonstrating the reality of it when Renton was rolling around under his duvet like a feeding crocodile while being attacked by malevolent wall-crawling toddlers. But that was the short version. The real deal lasts a lot longer and feels seven-and-a-half times worse than it looks.

Three hours to flight time, and I've just washed down the last of the tablets with a gulp of lukewarm water from a plastic bottle that was left behind on the table beside me by one of my co-travellers. I would have bought my own water, but I'm skint. Being skint and chronically addicted to drugs is a way of life for most of my kind. And like most lifestyle choices, it has its pros and cons. This particular lifestyle offers up a combination of inescapable uncertainty mixed with a liberal dose of pervasive desperation. It's a fabulous motivator and helps the end user to compromise and override all of their core values while decimating their own humanness.

"Sonny boy... stop rabbling on about so much shite man... give it a fuckin rest... we're in trouble here!... it's you and me... and yoooou need to listen to meeeeee... man!.. Look......... We have three hours to go before the flight takes of....... eons of time... Eons I say!............ If we're not going back to swamp land to find some money and score, then at least take a look around at the mugs floating about the airport............... there must be something we can do for cash?................ C'mon sonny boy..................... get yer thinking cap on and let's go....................... c'mon man... the flight takes 11 hours 44 minutes to London from Johannesburg, man..................... 11 fuckin hours and forty fuckin four minutes... ....and then there's the trip home from London............... another couple of hours......................... are you fuckin mental? A couple of shitty methadone tablets won't get the job done...................... and me and you both know it sonny boy! .... C'mon man.................... please... we need to get something for this journey....................... please sonny boy... please... ....even alcohol................... that'll

do!................................. it's better than fuck all...c'mon....c'mon....c'mon...let's go ....!!!!!..................!!!!! Move, ya fuckin prick! "

The final round of tablets have hit the spot, so I'm feeling a little less skitzy than usual. Must be the lack of crack over the past couple of days, combined with the slow release and long-acting nature of the tablets. Problem is, it's nowhere near long-acting enough. I've got about two hours max before the all-to-familiar creepy crawly swarm wakes up looking for the guy who poked its nest with a burning stick dipped in dog shit. I need a plan. I can't go backward. Those stabbing bandits were members of the 28's, and they're not the type to let me get away with wounding one of their tribe.

The 28's are a South African prison gang, and their counterparts are the 26's and 27's. They're known as the numbers gangs, and they make their American equivalents look like proper fannies. This gang's story began back to the 1800's when white South African coal mine owners used black people to do their dirty work for less than no money at all. A couple of disgruntled employees decided to set out on their own as full-time robbers. So, they looted and robbed the mine owner's properties wherever and whenever they could. Over the years, they grew and split into three different factions, all with their own special abilities and quirky predilections. The 26's are the thieves and money-makers, but they don't do violence. The 27's do all the violence. It's gratuitous and there's plenty of it. They also mediate in times of conflict between the different gangs. The 28's are the most feared. They're known as the night people. Their famous party trick is to slice the arseholes of gang members who misbehave and then one of the gang leaders, who is HIV positive, rapes them. Nice. The 26's run the show and control everything throughout the day, then hand the baton over to the 28's for the night shift. If the 28's catch me, they'll jamb that baton up my hoop just for entertainment purposes. And as an encore, they'll phone their pals in the 27's who'll pop down to shanty town and torture me to death and then toss me in the nearest river. The withdrawal induced crocodile-feeding analogy will become my reality.

So, it's back to Blighty we go, just as soon as I can rustle up enough dough for an alcohol-infused detox that is.

"Right, Sonny boy……….here's the plan………..listen up……..!"

Brent

Brent was frothing with delicious anticipation. He was going out with Eileen tonight. Usually, she only allowed him to see her on Tuesdays and Thursday's and Saturday's. It was Wednesday. A treat indeed. His expectations were very very high. The change of plans might mean that they would play his favourite game. He was sure of it. She didn't exactly say it, but he was convinced that the time was near because of the way she was moving and looking at him lately. Tonight is the night, he hoped. He stopped himself from thinking about it. He couldn't risk getting too excited when he was walking through the centre of town. "Must stay in control of that" he muttered to himself. To keep himself from indulging in those wonderful thoughts, just in case someone noticed, he reaffirmed his total commitment to his work and started reciting one of his self-fashioned mantra.

I am the knight ride-ahhhh!

I am the dark destroy-ahhhh!

I am the black mamb-ahhhh.

I am sleek and slick and I move in the shadoooowssss-ahhh

I will seek you out, wherever you ahhhhrrr!

You think you are smart. But I am smart-ahhhh!

You think you can escape me. But you are doooooomed!

You will not see me, but I will see you-ahhhh!

Where are you?

IS THIS TRUE

I will find you!

Where are you-ahhhh?

I will find you!

Where are you-ahhhh?

Where are you?

You think you can escape me -ahhhh!

But I will seek you out and I will find you-ahhhh!

Ahaaaaa! There you ahhhhrrr! I have you now. There is no escape from the dark destroyer-ahhhh!

"36952 Mckenzie to control, over" sshhhhhhhhhhh!

"36952 Mckenzie to control, over" squelchhhhhhhh!

"Yeah ok Brent, we know it's you. What do you want this time, and make it snappy, over"

"Ehhhhh, pardon me control-ahhhhh. Could you use my serial number and surname when communicating over the company's radio system. Remember company protocol-ahhh, over"

"Fuck off Brent, you absolute bell-end. What do you want, and make it quick"

"Ehhhh, excuse meeeee control. I must object. Strenuously-ahhh. I must inform you, once again, that I will be notifying management due the use of foul language over the company's radio system. This, as you well know-ahhh, is a serious breach of policy –ahhh! Over"

IS THIS TRUE ?

"For fuck's sake Brent. It's my fucking company. I own it. I'm the top of the tree. I'm your boss. Will you just give it a rest, you ding-dong? How many times do we have to go through this shite? You're a fucking part-time traffic warden, working for a private fucking parking control company. And I don't give a fuck about your other part-time job as a community police officer either, so don't start threatening me again with that one either. And you had better not be wearing that police issue stab-proof-vest on duty again. Now, what do you want? Jesus! Over.'

Kischhhhhhhhh…"36952 Mckenzie to control, I think I have a serious offender in my sights. Could you check the ANPR system for licence plate HG58 DBS, that is Hotel, Golf, Fiver, Eight, Delta, Bravo, Sierra. Ahhh, over.

"Lord, please help me. Yes yes, alright Brent. Alright. You're right. That car is six minutes overdue in parking bay 3-427. Now, you know we need to give each car owner ten minutes grace Brent. So calm you're passion, and don't put a ticket on it until then, over"

"Ahhh……Roger that control. Roger that. Ahh…36952 McKenzie, over and out"

Yes. Yes. Yes. Yes. Yes. Yes. Oh Yes –ahhhh! Brent has you now. There is no escape from the caped crusade-ahhhh. Yooooooou are mine now.

Three minutes to go, and you are all mine.

Come on, come on, nearly there. Nearly there. Yes, yes, here we go. Fifteen seconds.

"Oi you! Dickhead. Hold on. Don't you dare put a ticket on

IS THIS TRUE

I am the dark destroy-ahhhh!

I am the black mamb-ahhhh.

You think you can escape me -ahhhh!

But I will seek you out and I will find you-ahhhh!

Ahaaaaa! There you ahhhhrrr! I have you now. There is no escape from the dark destroyer-ahhhh!

"36952 Mckenzie to control. Over ahhh!"

Kevin

Bang, bang, bang.

"RIGHT YOU! WAKEY WAKEY, COCK WOMBLE. You've got court in 15 minutes, and you'll want to wash that sick and dried bold of your face before you go up in front of the Magistrate. Otherwise, you'll probably get remanded"

"Fuck off boss. I'm up."

I'm engaged in activity that most people would call thinking. This is not your everyday type of thinking. This is not the kind of thinking that the guy in the famous Greek statue does while he grinds his knuckles into his forehead. This is the frenzied version of thinking; the kind that usually follows a three-day crack binge. But I've been crack-less for days. I'm thinking, what the fuck happened? I'm thinking, how did I end up in a police cell? I'm thinking, how did I ended up in the UK, when the last thing I remember is waiting for a plane from South Africa? I'm thinking, where did the blood came from? I'm thinking, where is the stink of shit coming from? I'm thinking, where are my clothes? I'm thinking, do I look presentable in this white, paper, police-issue jumpsuit. I'm thinking, when are my withdrawal symptoms gonna kick in?

"Oi Boss. What am in for?"

"You're in big trouble mate. The last person who did what you did got ten years. Big trouble, no doubt about it stinky"

"Please Boss, don't fuck about man. What have I done? What am I in for?

"Wait and see cock womble, wait and see. You're booked to

see the duty solicitor in five. She'd better hope that she's got a clothes peg for her nose, pongo".

Fucking duty sergeants and their minions. This is not the first time I've woke up in a police cell and not known what I've done or how I ended up here. The sadistic twats like to play that game with their little-inebriated inmates, especially if they were given a hard time during booking. They try to frighten you into believing that you've committed a really bad crime when you were off your nut on drugs and that you're set for a big sentence when the judge gets his mitts on you. They think it's funny. But then, they would. I can't imagine that they have that much to laugh about in any other part of their lives.

"I need to see a doctor boss. I'm a drug addict and I'm susceptible to fits and seizures".

Got him. I know my way around the system and he's duty bound to meet my request. Back in the eighties and early nineties, he could just fuck me off and tell me that I was a junky scumbag and I deserved everything I got. That lasted until the corpses started to pile up in police cells and prisons across the country, mostly due to the heroin epidemic and resultant withdrawal-induced suicides. Heads rolled in the judicial system, and it's leaders were was forced into action, if only to stem the high cost of buying so many body bags. So, no such luck today for you, mister Tomás de Torquemada. The tables turned, and his tone changed as his keychain chimed.

"Oh right… ehhhh… right… Mr… ehhh… oh… we didn't get your name because of the condition you were in and we had to lock you up for your own safety… eh… right… I'll get the addictions liaison worker to come see you right away and I'll call the doc and we'll put your court appearance off until this afternoon. Eh… do you want some water or a cuppa?"

"What am I in for boss?" I said in my best authoritative voice, the one I use when I know that my opponent is on the ropes.

"Oh, it's not that bad son, just a bit of a scuffle on the aeroplane. We had to restrain you for your own good. You were in a bad way son. Do you take sugar?"

Police. Most of them are the same. Fuckers.

"Fuckinnnnn told you sonny boy… how many times?... but noooooooo … don't listen, do you? How many times have I warned you about alcohol……. Same result every time………. Wasting my time sonny boy…….. wasting my fucking time…………………. right the doc's due.   You know the dance … the dried blood, sick and stink of shit has turned into an opportunity………, opposed to a mere inconvenience, sonny boy……………… listen up … here's the plan… inbound drug courier arriving shortly and we're gonna fleece him……………… good 'n proper…"

The drugs liaison worker has just turned up, and she isn't half bad looking at all. We're exchanging pleasantries and playing the game. We both know that she doesn't have anything that interests me. She's a stereotypical drug worker. Those types have a distinct modus operandi, and it's is all about helping someone whose life is in a worse state than theirs. They are able to go home at night after a day's work, if you could call it that, believing that they've helped some poor unfortunate. That gives them licence to gurgle down a bottle and a half of wine every night and it solidifies the big fat lie that underpins and supports their existence. That lie is simple. It's "Well at least I'm not that bad." They sit at home, half-pissed most nights, and think about the lost souls that they are supposed to have helped. I've heard them regurgitate drivel like, "There for the Grace of God," and all that. We go through the motions, where I tell her a sob story and she swallows it. She fills in the necessary forms and ticks the appropriate boxes before telling me that the doc will be along soon. Drugs workers. Most of them are the same. Fuckers.

Fifteen minutes have passed and the doc has turned up. He isn't half bad looking at all. We're exchanging pleasantries and playing the game. We both know that he has access to everything that interests me. He's a stereotypical doctor who gets paid an exorbitant hourly rate and call-out fee to run around police cells dishing out doses of drugs to the needy, greedy and potential noose nuggets. Those types have a distinct modus operandi, (the GP's, not the junkies, although the junkies have distinct modus operandi too) but I've never been able to figure it out because of the power they have over me when I'm gagging for a fix. I think it's something to do with elitism and control but I can't be sure, because I'm gagging for a fix. What I am sure of, is that the doc and the drugs worker are employed by the State. And the State and its' employees keep giving me drugs if I ask for them, and then try to convince me that they have the answers to my problems because of their years of training and experience. It's difficult to take them seriously because they've just given me drugs, and they'll keep giving me them as a means to solving my drug problem. It's a bit like encouraging a drowning man to drink a cup of water. There can only be two reasons for such ludicrous thinking. Either the State drug system, and it's disher-outers, don't know what there are doing. Or they do, and they're keeping people hooked on prescription drugs as a perverse incentive that keeps the system turning over its allocated £1billion pound budget every year. Right now, the politics are a side issue because the doc's wise to me. I'm trying every trick in the book to get as much of anything and everything as I can. But he's seen it and heard it all before, and he's having none of it. He just coughed up the right amount of opiates and benzos to stop me from fitting and halt the onset of full-blown withdrawals. It has done nothing for my overactive thinking gland. GP's working in the drugs field. Most of them are the same. Fuckers.

"Sonny boyyyyy……… sonny boyyyyyyy……….. what the fuck was that? You lame fucking limpet………… a scraggy 20 mls of methadone and a couple of blues... is that fucking it? …………….. your losing your touch, sonny boyyyyyyoh... how many times do I need to tell you………….. listen to me………………. for fucks fucking sake..."

The drugs I received from the doc did the trick. Just. Time to see the magistrate and get of this dump. Here he comes. This lot are all the same, too. Fuckers. This one's looking decidedly iffy though. He's got a bit of squint eye going on and if I'm not mistaken, he's sporting a comb-over job, over a comb-over job. On the other hand, it might just be an unkempt wig. Whatever it is, it's threatening to fall over his good eye and into his glass of Robinsons squash. He takes a noisy slurp of his juice and gives me the glad eye, just before he launches a tirade of abuse at me for my escapades on the plane. This is all news to me. I can't figure out whether to believe him or burst out laughing. The fucker's got a lisp. As if his wonky eye and tilting syrup wasn't bad enough. Adding more insult to his injuries, he's talking almost exclusively through his nose. It makes him sounds like an angry goose bleating a car-horn.

"Mithter Wilkinthon," he spat, with no added sugar. "Your behaviour on the jet from thouth Africa was abtholutley appalling. You're a disgraith to yourthelf and to your country". Flick flick go the hairpieces, and winkety wink goes the other eye. My hyperactive thinking disorder kicks in, and this time its saying, "Please don't laugh. Somebody help me. Please don't laugh. Somebody help me. Please don't laugh." While I'm doing my best to hold it together, the magistrate continues his assault. "You should be thoroughly, thoroughly ashamed of yourthelf, I thay," he says, while strangely pointing his middle finger at me, when he should be using his index. I'm still thinking I'm not gonna make it here. I'm gonna go. I know it. "Please help me not to laugh."

He's oblivious, as he hit's full pelt. "I have in front of me an account of your behaviour, written by the pilot and hith flight thtaff Mithter Winkinthon. And I think you need to hear it, indeed I do. Firtht of all, the thouth African airport thecurity team report that you thtole a bottle of White Horth whithkey from duty free, and you conthealed it on your perthon before boarding the plane. Then, after the plane took off, it ith alleged that you drank the thaid withkey, very quickly indeed. The cabin crew, mithter Wilkinthon, were keeping an eye on you becauth they were contherned about your phythical appearanth. You theem to have had been shabbily dresthed and had thome thort of bandage wrapped around your neck. They thaid your complexion wath yellow, and you were thweating profuthley as you gulped down the withkey. It appearth that you fell athleeep, and the cabin crew removed the remainder of the withkey and dithcarded it down the think.

You theem to have drank around half of it, mithter Wilkinthon, and after about two hourth you awoke thcreaming and bawling, accuthing the cabin crew of theft. The cabin crew thaid you were deliriouth, and you theemed almotht thychotic. After trying to apeath you and calm you down, you then began thrashing your armth around, and it seemth that you hit one of the stewardethes in the eye. For your thake, you'd better hope her thight ith not impaired and there ith no lathting damage. When you couldn't get the thtaff to return your withkey, you stared convulthing and foaming at the mouth, as if you were taking thome thort of fit. Then, the staff thaid, your body thtiffenend and both of your legth shot our thtrait in front of you while you were making thome thtrange grunting and moaning noitheth. Upon which, mither Wilkinthon, you protheeded to defecate in you panths. Apparently the thmell was appalling, and the thtaff and other pathengers were left gagging and retching. Thome of theem to have vomited into the middle isle in dithgust. Ath if that'th not bad enough, you then began pulling and hauling at your belt and trouthers and thcreaming that you had been thabotaged in some way. Recounting your wordth, the thtaff claim you were hollering about a voice that livth in your head, and how it had fouled your panths when your back wath turned becauthe you didn't do what it told you at the airport. It theems that you eventually got out of your trouthers and pushed them under the theat in front of you with your feet, while you thtill had shoeth and thocks on and they were covered in feathes. The pathengers who occupied thoth theats were thent thcreaming into the theats in front of them, and this thtatred what can only be dethcribed as an avalanche of pathengerth fighting to get over each other and away from the horrendouth thtench. The remainder of the passengerth, who were unaware of your anticth, thought that the plane wath going to crash, and they were hithterical with fear. All of a thudden, inexplicably, you fell fast athleep for the remaining thix hours of the flight. You didn't even thtir when the polith dragged you from the plane. Now the polith inform me that you only awoke thith morning and the drugth liathon worker and the doctor tell me that you have abtholutley no memory of theth eventh. Do you have anything to thay for yourthelf, mithter Wilkinthon?

Who does this fucker think he is......... eh....... thonny boy!........ Lispy, comb-backed cunt.......... are you gonna let this turd get away with speaking to you like that... ....you're losing your fuckin touch sonny boy................. me and you................... sonnny boy............. always has been............. no doubt............ it's about time we gave this pokey middle-fingered fanny a taste of his own medicine. .... Trying to put the blame me for the shite escapade............... as if... sonny boy............. GET... HIM... FUCKING... TOLD... sharpish .... give him both barrels..................... booooooom!

"Yes, I would like to say something for myself. Not wanting to seem impolite or uninformed, I'm not sure how I should address you in court. As you are a magistrate, do I call you your honour?" I know fine well how to address this snivelling creep of creature, but I've got to back him up a bit or he'll stop me from having my say. "You call me Thir, or magithtrate, mithter Wilkinson. I prefer magithtrate," he honked. "Yes, your Magistrate", I said, without laughing. "Jutht magithtrate mither Wilkinthon, jutht magithtrate." I need to be careful here, he's zooming in on my sarcasm.

IS THIS TRUE ?

"Magistrate, as you know I travelled on the flight from South Africa. And, as you know, I had a bandage around my neck. That bandage was a dressing to treat a near fatal stab wound that I received as a victim of one of the most notorious gangs in that godforsaken country. The wound was treated in what I can only describe as a less than hygienic institution, in the middle of a ghetto in Cape Town. I can only surmise that my unexplainable and uncharacteristic behaviour came about due to an infection that I picked up in that awful place, which then led to some sort of delirium-oriented episode. Combined with this your honour, I'm sorry, Magistrate, you will see by me records that I have been a habitual injecting drug addict for nearly fifteen years. This tortuous lifestyle has left me with several blood-borne viruses, including hepatitis B and C. That's why I look so yellowish. By God's good grace, I seem to have avoided HIV and AIDS. Again, and I can only surmise, these infections must have further contributed to my delirious state and the accompanying bizarre behaviour." He's falling for it. He's sat back in his seat rubbing his chin, trying to figure out if I'm serious or taking the piss. I need to press on. "I understand that my previous history is appalling, Magistrate. And I'm sure you have sight of my antecedents, and a record of all of my previous custodial sentences for drug related offences. Magistrate, my motivation to leave South Africa was my deep desire to come home to the UK and change my ways, for good this time. I'm willing to do whatever it takes, to give up the drugs and reunite with my family and friends. I'm sure we both agree, that it's time for me to take responsibility for my actions. To stand up and be accountable, so to speak."

Well done sonny boy……… nice one……… nice one………. I think we're on for a community order here……… so, its straight to the clinic for a big script right after this................. but not before we get a clean set of clothes, some cash and a liberal dose of our favourite tipple................ sonny boy............ well done... well done.

"I mutht thay, mither Wilkinthon, that I'm thumwhat imprethed with the account you've given of yourthelf and the thircumthtanthes that led to the epithodie on the flight from thouth Africa. You theem like an intelligent individual, which leavth me wondering why you are in thuch a terrible condition. However, due to the theriousneth of the offenth in quethtion, I can't dethide whether to give you a cuthtodial thentence, or a community order." Wink, wink. Flick flick.

C'mon ya dodge-pot poof........... community order........... community order... me and my man need to get to fuck out of here............ quick style............ there's good old British gear to be got............ and we need to get some ... so stop pissin' about... you know it's the right thing to do ... a community order is the way to go............... ain't that right, sonny boyohhhhhh...!

"Ok mithter Wilkinthon, you've thwayed me. A community order it ith."

"Yesssssssss sireeee... Bob, sonny boy.........told you.... ... didn't I....... told you I knew what I was doing........ free prescription drugs....... ... for me and you....... always has been .... always will be........ we're outa here in fifteen minutes and we're gonna get fucking ... S M A S H E D....... Yessssssss....... now, no fucking about sonny boy......... listen to me........... keep up the good work and let wank chops think he's got the better of us............ wot a fukin pleb...!

"My dethithion in this inthtance, mithter Wilkinthon, ith to thentence you to a compulthory abthtineth baithed rethidential rehabilitation thentre for twelve monthhh. Pierpoint Houth, in Black pool. I will arrange for you to be tranthpoted directly there from here, today. You will not be releathed into the community today and if you fail to meet thith order, you will be thent directly to prithon for eighteen monthhh. Do you underthtand, mithter Wilkinthon ?"

AHHHHHHHHHHHHHH!....... Sonny boyyyyyyy.........! No fucking way.......... get that cunt told......... do something......... fucking abstinence based residential rehabilitation centre................ what's that supposed to even mean?.......... please sonny boy................ do something....................... throw something at him... where's those shit covered socks and shoes?................ stink bomb the bastard................ get us sent down................ fucking rehab... fucking compulsory abstinence............. it's Pierpoint House, for fucks sake............. we've heard about that place............. you can't let this happen sonny boy............. contempt the fuck out of this court and that skinny dying bastard of a magistrate............... AHHHHHHHHHHHHHH................ sonny boy............... fucking do something... quick... please...!

I don't really fancy a stint in jail. I don't really fancy going back home either to see that mob of a family. Maybe rehab might not be so bad?

"Sonny boy... what the fuck man... don't think like that... you'll get us killed... please sonny boy... don't... I'm begging you!"

"Thank you, magistrate. I agree. I don't think incarceration would help me this time. I believe the court has made a good decision, and again, I can't thank you enough"

"Very well mithter Wilkinthon. I will arrange with the bailiff, thocial thervices and probation to have you tranthfered thith afternoon. Now, if I thee you in my court again, I will have you thent down for ath long ath pothible. Goodbye, mithter Wilikithon."

"Thank you, magistrate. Oh. Magistrate, could I address the court one last time before I go."

"If you mutht, mithter Wilkinthon. If you mutht"

"Thank you again. At the beginning of proceedings, magistrate, you said that I was a disgrace to myself and my country, and that I should feel ashamed. I would like to respond to that. Is that ok?".

"I thuppose tho, mither Wilikinthon. But make it brief".

"Thank you. In respect to myself and the other passengers, I regret the incident on the plane, but I do not feel ashamed or disgusted. In reality, I see myself as a person who is fundamentally unwell. I have no idea why I do the things I do. Perhaps this spell in rehab will afford me the opportunity to find out. As for feeling ashamed about my country, I cannot, because I am not a nationalist. To be ashamed, I would need to be proud to be British, and I'm not. I do not align myself with this ideology in any way. You see, Magistrate, nationalism is no different from other types of identity badges, like religion, sexual orientation, football team, gender, race, class distinction, personal wealth, job title, fashion and fads, creeds, gang memberships, tribalism, secret societies or political alliances. The list goes on and on. As far as I'm' concerned, most people want to, or need to know themselves within the parameters of one or a multitude of these ridiculous ideas and beliefs. Otherwise, they would feel utterly insignificant, in every sense of the word. Unbeknown to them, a problem occurs every time they choose one or more of these identities. When someone choses to be a Muslim, or British, or a Freemason or whatever, they automatically create and inherit an opposite. No matter how they try to disguise it, this opposite, in reality, becomes 'the other.' In other words, the enemy. If this opposite or enemy, did not exist, they would not be able to maintain this view of themselves. Without this opposite, they would cease to be what and who they think they are. It makes simple sense. A person who identifies themselves as black, for example, cannot know themselves without a white, or other some other coloured person to compare and judge himself or herself against. Ahhhhh, I see what you're thinking, Magistrate. You're thinking that being black, or any other colour is not a choice. Of course it is. The colour of someone's skin is not a choice, that's obvious. I'm talking about a choice to be identified by the colour of their skin, or their job or social status or whatever. You know the list. A member of the Aryan brotherhood needs his skin colour to be who he is, just the same as a Chinese person need his to be Chinese. Do they not? Ahhhhh, I can see what you're thinking now, Magistrate. You're thinking that people don't make 'informed choices' to be a certain race, or creed or religion, or any other mythical notion. And you'd be right. They don't make 'informed choices,' because they are only afforded one option, and they must choose it or perish. Let me explain. Small children don't understand such concepts, do they? Through time, they develop awareness of themselves and their surroundings. During this time, they are taught to be whatever the people around them are. At this point of teaching, they must choose to be the same as their teachers or suffer the consequences, and I'm sure you can imagine what those consequences look like. More often than not, this choice-less choice is offered up under the facade of dogmatic philosophies such as family, culture, heritage and country of origin, and so on. So, Magistrate, I wonder if your scathing judgements on my character and your idea of what I should and should not be, was an attempt to coerce me into making one of these choice-less choices. Or, did you feel your own shame and disgust because you unknowingly aligned yourself with me. After all, you unwittingly branded me British? If this is the case, should I apologise to you personally for offending your sense of who and what you think you are? And apart from all that, who would want to be British anyway? It's hardly a badge of honour, your honour. Is it?"

"MITHTER WILKINTHON. HOW FUCKINGGGGGG DARE YOU?"

Oooooh...touchy. Looks like his Magistrate has just heard his own voice and noticed the droplets of orange squash spewing from his lispy lips. He's looking around the room in a state of panic for someone to blame. No joy today, your Magistrate. That was all you, and no-one else. I'm having a good look around the room too, but just to gauge the audience's response. Tuts and huffs and eyes to the ceiling abound. They are not best-pleased with his Magistrate's outburst, and it looks like a few of them are on their phones trying to gain pole position on Facebook. Lots of kudos to be gained from being the first to share this juicy news with as many people as possible. This is "likes" nirvana. Looks like a few more have hit the video record button as well, and they're going for

IS THIS TRUE ?

YouTube glory as well. Priceless. He's trying to regain his composure, and his reverse lights are beeping like fuck. Limply, he stutters "Ehhhhhh, Mithter Wilkinthon, I hold you in contempt of court. Cough, cough, wink and flick. You manipulated me into believing that you were therious about changing the courth of your life, but all the time you were planning thith little charade". Then he turns the volume back up, as he begins to forget about his little faux pas. "YOU are a deviant, thir. If I had not already pathed thentence, I would thend you thtraight to prithon. BAILIFF, take thith cretin out of my thight." And up and off he storms, out of the chambers. I'm half expecting to have a limp. But no such luck.

As soon as he's out of the room, the phones are revving up and their owners are fixated on their screens and tapping like Billy Oh. Fuck it. I'm off to rehab. Let's see what this lot in Blackpool have to say for themselves. My spine spasms once again, signalling the onslaught of the creepy crawly brigade. This is gonna be rough.

"Please sonny boy... don't."

"Shut the fuck up you."

Cheryl and Eileen.

Eileen was treating herself to a new outfit along with a trip to the hairdressers and beauty salon. She was meeting Brent tonight, but that had nothing to do with her treat. It was Wednesday. That was all the reason she needed. Cheryl agreed to go with her and was upstairs putting the finishing touches to her look. A few minutes earlier, Eileen had booked a taxi. Cheryl was keeping Eileen waiting.

"Hurry up Cheryl. The taxi's coming."

"I'm sorting my make up!"

Would you just do it Cheryl" sniped Eileen from the foot of the stairs. "All the wondering and pondering in the world never gets anything done. How…Many…Times? "Ayyy…Ceeee…Teeee…Eye…Ohhhh…Ennnnn, Cheryl. Action, action." She enunciated, and every syllable was tinged with her own brand of caustic sarcasm.

A-C-T-I-O-N was one of the monotonously repetitive quotes that Eileen claimed she came up with in a moment of divine inspiration. But like the rest of her cues and sayings, of which there were far too many to count, it was pirated. If anyone ever challenged her about the source of these words, she would immediately mutilate their character. All challengers were fair game if they dared question her integrity and authority on any subject at all. In the interest of personal safety, it was best to placate her and force a smile.

"Let's go Cheryl. The taxi's coming and the shopping is not going to do itself now, is it?"

"OK, OK OK, I'm coming," Cheryl screamed. Then under her

breath and out of earshot she muttered, "for fucks sake." She was adept at muttering and complaining just outside the range of Eileen's radar-like earwigging skills. At a recent dinner party, someone chanced telling a little joke about it. They said, "Eileen could hear the grass grow, and she would probably say that she was the original author of that saying too!". No one laughed, just in case Eileen was in range and heard them. They knew very well that she would make them pay.

"Cheryl. Cheryl!" barked Eileen, in a foreboding tone that she used to let listeners know she was on her way to serious city. She did not like to be kept waiting. Not at all. "Cheryl, you're doing it again. Every time. Every time. How many times Cheryl? You know how I feel when you make me late or make me wait. Why do you do this to me? Why Cheryl? Why? After everything that I've done for you. After Everything. You make me wait and make me late. Again, and again and again, Cheryl. You know how this makes me feel. It's not as if I haven't told you. Is it? Come on!"

To Cheryl, this was all too familiar. It was another one of their "things". If she could bear the sickening mass that filled the pit of her stomach every time her mother started on her like this, she would take a moment to touch and feel the weight of it and her mother's jibes as they pulled her guts towards her feet. If she could mange this, just once, she would respond and give life to the words that accompanied her feelings. If she could, she would say what she really wanted to say her. She would scream the screams, and she would feel the fire in her throat as she let rip at last. But she was bewildered and had no idea how to do it. So she swallowed and stalled, and made her mother wait a little longer. Making her mother wait was the best she could do to defend herself in times like these. At least it was something, she thought.

"Last time Cheryl. Last time" squawked Eileen.

The taxi arrived. At the last minute, Cheryl came downstairs to find her mother's stare and tight mouth. She was holding the front door open. They closed the door behind them and walked down the path to the waiting cab. They opened the cab door and both sat in the back seat. Eileen gave the driver directions. For the next three or four minutes, they sat in total silence. Silent sessions were another one of their "things." Who would speak first? There were no rules in this game. No matter which way it went, Eileen knew she was right. On the other hand, she didn't know how to be wrong. Being wrong was for other people. What was the point of that? Cheryl knew she was right, but felt wrong. Feeling wrong was a constant companion that lurked in her shadow. When her mother was near, it became more noticeable. She knew that arguing with her mother was fruitless. In fact, she knew that arguing with her mother would make matters worse. Whenever she stood her ground and argued her point to the finish, she always ended up boiling with rage and storming off for a few days. When her anger subsided, she vowed to stay away for good. But, she couldn't. An overwhelming force with the feel and texture of glutinously acrid syrup kept drawing her back. To save herself from the repetitive drama, Cheryl broke silence and said, "I'm thinking of having some work done. Lip fillers and little bit of Botox?." Instantly Eileen said, "That's a great idea. There's nothing wrong with a little enhancement. It's just the same as wearing makeup. These things aren't permanent, so they're harmless. Is it expensive?" "It's not too bad." Replied Cheryl. "I can afford it, and Oslo gave me some money for my birthday." As the conversation moved on, Cheryl's anger faded into the distance to join forces with her sense of wrongness in the background. For now, they were a team again. They were mother and daughter on day out in town. For the rest of the day, their focus of attention was on other people. Especially the ones who deserved their judgement and condescension. To round the day off, Eileen surprised Cheryl by taking her for lip fillers and the Botox injections she was after. As usual, they snapped photos of their new clothes, haircuts and makeovers for Facebook-time later on. Their "friends" would tell them how beautiful they looked, and that they looked like sisters opposed to mother and daughter. Eileen loved that.

Jumping Jack

He ran across the full length of the bed as fast as he possibly could. There was no intention to decelerate or to gauge the distance between himself and his jumping-off point. He didn't need to be convinced that there was enough space left to plant his foot and launch himself into the air. He just did it. And he did it with all the gangly style and flailing grace of a colobus monkey when it makes death-defying leaps across impossible distances from tree to tree. To him, the gap between his take-off point and his intended landing pad was of no consequence. He hadn't developed concepts like reasoning, or calculation and risky yet. These things were of no use to him. As time passed, these ideas and many more like them would be forced upon him anyway, whether he liked it or not. In the near future, he wouldn't be asked if he would like to consider the ideas or to take some time to think about them and return to discuss the matter sometime later. His future teachers and mentors would compel him into believing that these things were indispensable facts of life; that he needed to agree with them to ensure his safety and future successes as a good and prosperous person. He was heading into a world where his teachers would convince him that he needed to learn and obey all of his society's rules and norms and that they must be adhered to at all times, otherwise the consequences would be dire. But, he was in mid-flight. So, none of that mattered. As he came into land, he instinctively opened his arms and legs at the same time. When he reached his target, he wrapped his arms around her neck and his legs around her waist. He clung to her back like a limpet. He beamed in his victory over the forces of gravity and he basked in the glory of another successful adventure. And he smiled. And his smile had enough energy to light up a small Austrian village in the middle of a winter blackout. Natalie, his mother, didn't seem to register the fact that she had just inherited an additional 15 kilogrammes of clinging limpet with curly hair and an exaggerated sense of accomplishment. She was too busy picking up dirty laundry and tidying away toys that were destined to reappear on the floor behind her in about fifteen minutes. When that time came, she would look puzzled and wonder if she hadn't just put them away a moment earlier. Then, she'd blow a deep exhale to convince herself that she was wrong and retain her sanity for one more day. Natalie hadn't really failed to acknowledge the arrival of the little jockey on her back, who was now even happier because he had a horse. She knew fine well he was there. But she did something that is quite rare for a capitalist-modern-day-mother. And it's not something that can be learned or taught. In spite of her obvious frustrations with a messy house and two other children aged nine and fifteen running amok indoors on a school holiday, she was able to celebrate his triumphant escapade with him. At the same time, she acknowledged her annoyance at everything else. In spirit, Natalie was blessed with the ancient wisdom and knowledge that allowed her to hold her anger and her love simultaneously. Instinctively, she knew where both feelings originated and where they belonged. She didn't get mixed up and blame Jack. Little Jack was aware that his mother was peeved, but he knew that it wasn't directed at him. She would never let Jack, or any of her children, think that they were somehow responsible for her feelings unless it was absolutely appropriate and correct to do so. She would never tell them to go watch TV or to play outside because she was too busy. Or make them wait for her attention because she was talking to a friend on the phone. Or berate them for disturbing her while she was engrossed in some meaningless Facebook trivia. Not that she has a Facebook account anyway, which only makes her more of an anomaly among modern mothers. She wouldn't accuse them of scaring her because they unconsciously wandered off into the street. Or tell them she would leave them behind if they didn't hurry up. Or tell them that Santa won't leave them presents unless they behaved. Or scold them for writing with crayons on the walls.

She wasn't one of those parents who use any of the innumerable blaming, bullying or scare tactics that are disguised as teaching methods. She knew that these strategies didn't help the child. She knew that they only made the adult's experience a little less painful. Natalie was not of that ilk. Her character was made of something totally different. And that something was visible in the shine in the eyes and smiles of her young children. The most remarkable thing about Natalie is, that she is the way she is in spite of being Eileen's oldest daughter. Eileen is the way she is too. She has always been that way. She is unable to love and knows nothing of kindness or nurturing. On top of that, she is petty, cruel and uncaring. Yet so far, Natalie and her character survived her mother, seemingly unscathed.

Kevin

I'm engaged in an activity that most people would call simultaneously withdrawing from heroin and a mixture of other drugs in a rehabilitation centre in Blackpool. Like its opposite, using and abusing a combination of heroin and other drugs for sustained periods, it is a discipline that's reserved for the selected few. To be a player in this game, one must possess and entertain certain characteristics, ideas, ethics, and values. Above all else, self-loathing is paramount. If you don't have it, you can't play. My bones feel like they are under attack by a horde of gnawing parasites, armed with rusty cheese graters. My muscles are as tight, twisted and as bound as fossilised jungle vines. My saliva tastes of polecat piss. I've never tasted polecat piss, but I have whiffed it once or twice and my spit reminds me of the smell. The idea of the polecat piss is turning and churning my guts. Heroin is the king of constipation, (that sounds like I'm introducing a historically famous Athenian leader and the country he presides over) so I haven't had a proper shit for at least three weeks. The churning and turning are signalling the imminent arrival of a bag of goodies that will make the polecat piss smell like lavender water. When the shit show begins, the flavour of my slobber will undoubtedly change suit and I'll be able to taste the impending stench. I've been here before. I know that the arrival of the putrid pong will kick-start a deluge of dry retching and acrid vomiting. In the following minutes, hours and days, the cyclical nature of poo and spew will ensue. Eat your heart out, Wordsworth, Keats and TS Elliot. That's the thing about heroin withdrawal. It's a sort of comedic, poetic justice. Although right now, I'm not laughing. The crap and puke are set to arrive at the same time, so I'm worried about putting my arse or my face over the toilet bowl. It's a toss-up. Do I barf down the pan and shit on the floor, or vice-versa? The idea of cleaning up three-month-old fermented faeces doesn't appeal to me. It's just making me feel sicker, which is putting even more pressure on my shit-chute. This is a bad do. I'm gonna blow. As if that's not bad enough, my nervous system is shot to bits. Uncontrollable twitches and spasms are running up and down the length of my body. My head is bursting. Someone seems to have adorned it with an inside out, spike-laden Speedo cap. During the admission process, the rehab staff informed me that I won't be getting any methadone or benzo's for twenty-four hours because they need to be sure that I've not taken anything before I got here. They don't want an overdose on their hands. I tried to convince them by pleading that I didn't get a chance to score, because of my escapades on the plane from Africa and my little spell in custody. They're having none of it though. Most, if not all of the staff are ex-drug addicts themselves. There's no way past them. They've seen it, done it, and won the t-shirt. They've told me to call them "recovering addicts" opposed to "ex-drug addicts." Strange. Anyway, I can't get around them, and my detox regime won't start until I see the doctor tomorrow morning. Until then, it's a night on the splatter box for me. I need to go. NOW.

Oh, glory be to the man on highest. There's a sink right beside the bog pan. Looks like I won't be cleaning the floor after all. Keks down. Legs akimbo. Chin on the edge of the sink. Holding on with both hands. Here goes. Don't ask me why, but I've just started humming the Dambuster's theme tune. This is gonna hurt.

It's around 2 am. I've been given a solitary bed in the detox unit because they know I'll be up all night making lots of strange noises. They don't want me keeping the other residents awake. They're not wrong about the strange noises. After the first few bum chuffs and violent vomits, I seem to have passed out for a few minutes. The blood must have shot to my brain to quickly, due to the pressure release of all that pent-up dung. I came-to with my trousers around my ankles and a trail of dried sick smeared up the front of my nose and my forehead. That must've happened when I slid off the pan and my face dragged itself down the front of the sink. This is the second time in three days that I've woke up in the same state. Shit and sick figure strongly in both events. Surprisingly, there wasn't as much mess as there should have been. I cleaned myself up to the best of my ability and headed for the bed. That was about six hours ago. At 8 pm, a staff member popped her head in to see if I was OK. She wasn't half bad looking at all. I looked up at her and imitated a dying swan, so she just made some polite noises and gestures before setting off on her rounds. Before she went, she said she had visited some time earlier and told me that I was spinning deliriously around and around under the duvet. She said that I was crying out for someone called Jack and asking him to take me for a walk. I can't remember any of that. But I know who Jack is.

It's 8 am, and I'm due to see the doc at half past. That was a rough night.

"Sonny boy...stop ignoring me...............
please......................... let's just get a script from this doc and we'll blow this joint man....................... they're a bunch of frustrated hippy do-gooders man.....................
pretendy drug ddicts................... not like me and

you…theese fuckers don't know what a good habit is………………… fucking giro junkies man………………… c'mon sonny boy…………… let's go…………… me and you……………… none of them… don't tell them nothing…………… let's go…!"

"FUCK OFF   FUCK OFF   FUCK OFF   FUCK OFF   FUCK OFF   FUCK OFF

FUCK OFF   FUCK OFF   FUCK OFF   FUCK OFF   FUCK OFF   FUCK OFF

FUCK OFF   FUCK OFF   FUCK OFF   FUCK OFF   FUCK OFF   FUCK OFF"

A man pops his head around the door. "Kevin. Are you ok? Who are you shouting at?

"Eh. Oh. Sorry. I'm feeling a bit rough. I've not slept. I must be a bit delusional. Sorry. Sorry."

"It's OK Kevin. The doctor's here to see you. Downstairs. First door on the right."

"Thanks. Eh. Eh." I stutter.

"My names Mike. I'm the lead therapist here. I'm your designated counsellor. We'll have a chat later. Let's get your detox sorted first, eh."

"Yeah. Eh. Eh. Thanks. Eh Mike." I stutter again.

"Stutterin tit…………Keep away from that cunt sonny boy……………… he's bad news… shifty eyed old bastard…………… worth a' watching that one……………… right… let's do this doc over!"

"FUCK OFF YOU"

The docs an old man.

"Gooooooood……sonny boyyyyyy! He's our's……………We'll have the lot thanks…………………and a little bit more……………"

"WOULD YOU JUST FUCK OFF? I've had enough…."

"Hello doc"

"Hello son. Sit down. I'm here to prescribe you detox medication, which I'm sure you already know."

"I know doc, thanks."

"I need to make sure that you are titrated properly, to avoid any over-medicating issues. So, can you give me a brief history of your drug use? Just start from the beginning."

I'm all set. All primed. Ready to give the old doc the usual spiel. He looks pretty frail, and a bit shaky. I could have him over, no problem. He'll be eating out of my hand in no time. Something's up. I don't feel right. It's not the withdrawals. That's just an occupational hazard. As usual, they are horrendous but familiar. I'm looking at the old man and I don't want to tell him a pack of lies. He seems really kind. It's not like me to notice stuff like that. I usually see weakness and opportunity. Although, I'm remembering that I wasn't always like that.

"You OK, son?"

"I'm rough, doc. But no more than usual. I've been up spewing and shitting rings around myself all night.

Eh…Sorry, doc. No offence."

"None taken son. None taken. Now tell me about your drug history, and I'll sort your detox. You'll be able to get some medication in half an hour or so. It'll put you right. It's going to be OK son, you can get through this."

The old doc has piercing blue eyes with flecks of burnt orange running through the irises. It gives them a gold-ish appearance. They don't look as aged as he does. There's something else about him. It's his kindness. He looks as if he carries it wherever he goes, just in case someone needs some. I've never seen anything like this. I wish he would stop looking at me. He's not staring and he's not smiling. At the same time, he seems to be looking straight through me, and he's armed with happiness, sort of. I wish he'd stop looking at me. He's just sitting there. Looking. Nearly smiling. Nearly not. His cheeks are beetroot red. Not drunken, beetroot red. More, Santa-beetroot-red. He has a full head of pure white hair. I wish he would stop looking in me. Everything about him is relaxed. I wish he would stop looking into me. He's wearing a tweed jacket with leather elbow covers. I remember that I called those things geography teacher jackets when I was at school. I wish he would stop loo…..

I've broken down in the doctor's room.

I'm out of the chair.

I've slid onto the floor.

I'm weeping. Bawling.

I can hear myself.

I've never heard a noise like it.

I'm hammering at my chest with the heel of my hand.

My heart.

My heart is splitting.

My heart has split.

I have split.

Help me.

Help me.

My heart is split.

I'm howling. Wailing.

Help me.

I'm falling in.

Help me. Someone.

The old man is with me.

Smiling.

Help me Jack.

Walk with me.

Help me grandpa.

I can't stop.

I'm losing.

Help me.

Walk with me Jack.

Help me.

I'm lying cowered in a ball, on the floor. My eyes and throat are saturated with warm salty tears. I'm drowning. I'm going to drown in my own tears. I can't stop this. I'm drifting.

Help me Jack.

Walk with me.

Help me Jack.

Help me.

I'm hammering at my chest again.

Help me…A man's hand rests on the side of my head. It's a big hand. Big strong, sausage-like fingers. It's calloused and rough, from years of hard industrial labour. It's a warm hand. It's a loving hand. Jack is with me. I know it.

I'm slowing…

I'm slowing…

I'm falling…or floating…

I'm slowing…

I'm drifting…

I'm warming.

I'm sobbing. Softer…

Softer…

I'm warming…

I can hear my breath. I can feel my breath…

I'm sobbing and moaning… Or am I humming…?

I'm humming…

I'm warming. …

I'm drifting. Drifting… drifting… drifting… drifting… the warm hand…

Am I asleep?

Eileen

Occasionally, Eileen thought about Kevin. She wondered where he was or what he was doing. This annoyed her. She didn't want him in her head. It spoiled her mood. Especially tonight. She was in an unusually good mood, as she was getting ready to go out and meet Brent. She knew she was in good spirits because she had just caught herself humming and silently singing an old Rod Stewart tune called, "Tonight's the Night." Happiness and Eileen were incompatible. Like all other feelings, happiness arises in its own time and under its own steam. But for her, this emotion always felt like a blunt knife trying to find its way between her ribs. When she realised that this feeling was trying to visit, she did what she always did. She stamped her right heel into the ground below her, as hard as she possibly could. As always, it was always a calculated assault. She had practiced it a lot. The stomp was laden with the just right amount of authentic rage to get the job done. She knew how to hold back on the power, to avoid seriously injuring herself. On this occasion, it was a barefoot encounter with a solid hardwood bedroom floor. It smarted a little, and it may or may not bruise later on, she thought. But no real damage done. She smirked at herself and at her victory over such a loathsome emotion. Then she blew a chuff at the air, and another at the image of herself getting caught up in such frivolous behaviour. Thoughts of Kevin tried to renter the scene. She treated them with the same disdain

Eileen had been singing the words to that song in silence because she had vowed never to sing aloud again. This was due to an incident at a talent contest she entered in her early teens. In truth, she had a beautiful voice. Her mother, who was one of the sweetest people you were every likely to meet, had told her so on countless occasions. In spite of the insidious and sinister behavioural traits that Eileen had displayed since birth, her mother never tired of garnering all of her love and kindness and using it to try to change her daughter. She believed that her love could conquer Eileen's corrosive tendencies and that all she needed was enough time and patience to do so. Eventually, she thought, Eileen would soften, and her inborn character would yield. Every now and then, she would gently remind Eileen that she had a wonderful singing voice and that this was something she could use to bring happiness and comfort into the lives of other people. She was never pushy, and always mindful enough to ensure that her own needs, as a mother who wants to feel proud of her daughter, never got in the way or influenced her approach. Eileen's mother was remarkable in this way. She exemplified an unusual level of awareness and true compassion for her daughter, in spite of her overwhelming desire to dislike her. She knew, as all mothers know, that not all of her children were the same. And that this one was fundamentally unlikeable in every way. Undeterred, she would do everything she could to counteract nature's appetite for creating things both good and bad. In Eileen's case, it created bad.

Eileen's mother believed that encouraging her to sing in public might help her to connect with people in a different way, possibly resulting in a more positive exchange. That it might perhaps lighten her spirit, and make her more amenable to others.

She had seen and felt the reactions that most people had when they met her daughter; responses that were fleeting and almost unnoticeable to anyone else. Most displayed a sort of bewilderment and confusion, but the more sensitive types would recoil and scrunch their faces up as if they had just bumped into a foul smell. It was apparent to Eileen's mother that most people just didn't like her daughter, even if they had no reason not to. Eventually, Eileen succumbed to her mother's gentle encouragements to take up singing in public. It wasn't that she wanted to please her, or cooperate with her, or show her that she could be a good daughter and perhaps give her hope that they might be able to develop a good mother-daughter relationship someday. That was never going to happen. Some things are set in stone. It was to shut her up, once and for all about the singing. The talent show was scheduled to take place at the local community centre in six weeks' time. Eileen had developed a plan to ensure that it went as wrong as it possibly could. All she had to do was make sure that she drank enough water before the show. Half measures didn't suit her.

Eileen was fourteen years and two months old on the day of the talent competition at the community centre. The community centre was built in the 80's. It was typical for its time: a concrete, single–storey, multi-roomed building covered in bright white roughcast walls with a flat roof. All of it hemmed in behind a green, six-foot steel fence on a little piece of lost ground with a paltry carpark.

Eileen chose to sing the most difficult song she could think of. It was Whitney Houston's "I will always love you." She was aware that the song had been wrung out of all it's worth on every karaoke stage and televised and untelevised talent show since its release. But this didn't faze her. Her performance depended on the amount of water she was able to drink before the show. The song and the singing would be inconsequential.

Eileen's mother was filled with hope. This was her natural state. On this special evening, she was positively brimming with it. She felt as if she was making progress with this one of her children, at last. All her patience, tolerance, love, understanding and hard work over the years was about to bear fruit. Her daughter was blossoming, as every young adult should. She was on the verge of bursting with tears of joy and happiness.

It was Eileen's first time on stage, yet she didn't feel nervous or excited in the slightest. To her, it was all just matter of fact. Even at fourteen years old, she knew that she would never waste emotional energy on other people. What was the point in worrying about what the audience thought of her? She wasn't prepared to trade in that way. To her, all others were inconsequential, unless they possessed obvious benefits. Then she would trade with them. But her currency was counterfeit.. She would act as if a mutual exchange was taking place and convince the other that both parties would benefit equally from the interaction. But not so. Her methods were calculated. In later life, as an adult, she would become adept at making other people believe that they were being treated fairly and equally if she wanted something from them at the time. But soon afterwards, they would feel as if they had been stung, yet unable to recall tangling with anything venomous. She was young now and she knew it, but she was mastering that art of surreptitiously taking without giving. She was proud of that.

Eileen stepped forward on the stage for her big moment. She saw her mother sitting front and centre, right where she hoped she would be. She turned her head to the left and nodded to a stagehand who was ready to bring the music in on her cue. Eileen began to sing the acapella introduction to the song. Her voice was huge. It mimicked Whitney's to near perfection, and it kicked the audience back into their seats. Her mother's heart soared to new heights. When the introduction finished, the stagehand pushed the play button and the music chimed in perfectly. Eileen stopped abruptly. She appeared stunned, as she stared out into the audience with the facial expressions and body language of a shame-filled and fearful child. Then, she bent both legs slightly forwards until both knees were just touching each other. Following this, she placed her right hand in front of her genitals and she crossed her left arm over her newly formed breasts while her bottom lip and chin began to quiver. As soon as she managed to the squeeze the first round of tears from her eyes, she set the second part of her plan in action. She stood still and pissed herself on purpose. In that instant, she knew that it was a good plan, and she had executed it perfectly, so far. She also knew that it was foolproof. No one would ever expect that she had faked something like this. How could they?

Her mother was the first to notice the welling black stain as it spread across the front of the light blue jeans that she bought her for such a special occasion. Gradually, one-by-one, the audience cottoned on, and what began as low mumbled murmuring soon turned into a sea of pointing fingers and raucous laughter. Eileen burst into full-on sobbing and howling mode. This was the first time she had shown this tactic in public and it was a skill that she would hone and polish and use in the years to come. There was no doubt about her singing ability, but she had raw acting talent too. This gave her the ability to play out the rest of her plan in a scene that was worthy of an Oscar nomination. Feigning deeper shame and self-disgust, she threw both hands across her face. From the back of her interlaced finger-shaped mask, she peeked through with one eye to watch her mother reactions. "Bullseye", she hissed, through thin, tight lips.

Eileen's mother's world fell away. Eileen felt it go as it dropped, and she saw it in her face too. To accompany her kind and loving nature, her mother was blessed and cursed with naivety. And as it does with all people who are made this way, it blinded her from the darker side of humans and their nature, which in this case was her own daughter's enthusiasm for cruelty. In her eyes and heart, she was completely responsible for her daughter's plight. And all she could see and feel, was her daughter standing on stage, sobbing and soaked in her own urine, at the mercy of a ridiculing crowd. How could she have made such a mistake? She should never have encouraged her to sing in the first place, she thought. Instinctively, she sprung out of her seat and onto the stage and threw her arms and coat over her daughter's shoulders in an attempt to shield and shelter her from the exposure she faced. To complete her plan, Eileen stiffened her body in response to her mother's touch. In that stiffening, her mother sensed and felt something unfamiliar in Eileen. A phrase sprung to mind in reaction to this new sensation emanating from her daughter. It was, "cold lard". Internally she baulked at the idea. How could her daughter smell and feel like cold lard? As she stood there bemused at her own thoughts and feelings, Eileen lambasted her with a torrent of verbal abuse and blame. At the same time, she sharply extended both arms and slammed both of her palms into her mother's chest. Her mother reeled backwards, and stuttered and tottered on both heels towards the edge of the stage. Eileen almost burst out laughing because she thought she looked like an Irish dancer who had just failed an audition for Riverdance. She caught herself just in the nick of time and stifled the potential outburst. She reprimanded herself for her foolishness and reminded herself that she had an important role to play tonight. It would be catastrophic if anyone in the audience suspected she was acting. Her mother's heels clipped the edge of the stage and she fell hard, straight-backed and open-armed onto the hard, polished community centre floor three feet below. The back of her head met the wooden floor first and it cracked open. She lay unconscious. Eileen couldn't believe her luck. She didn't see that one coming, but took advantage of the situation immediately and turned the volume up, full blast. She began wailing and sobbing, and cried "oh no, look at what I've done. Please God, somebody help her. Pleeeeeeeeasseeeee!" The majority of the crowd gathered around to help her mother. A few came to Eileen also, and reassured her that it wasn't her fault, and that everyone had seen it, and it was an accident.

Forty-eight hours later, doctors said her mother was in a persistent vegetative state. In days gone by, she would have been called a vegetable. Eileen nearly cracked a sick joke on hearing the news. Once again, she instinctively shut herself up to avoid suspicion. Instead, she belted out another round of snot and sobs, and woes and wails. Two Oscar nominations in as many days.

At the funeral, Eileen stayed behind when everyone else left. As she stood at the foot of the grave, staring at the epitaph on the headstone, she thought she felt sadness beginning to rise up in her. On feeling it, she stamped her heel as hard as she could into the hard-packed ground beneath her feet and growled: "fuck that!"

On recalling these memories as she was getting ready for her date, she half-laughed and shouted aloud "Yeah, tonight's the night alright Brenty boy!"

Brutus, Cheryl and Oslo

What's that smell?

Cheryl and Olso are at it again. They've just heard about a supposed terrorist bombing in the city centre, and they're off to see what happened. Ghoulish, car-less rubberneckers. She's got me buckled and strapped into her "every-day bag". An old Moschino number that's past its sell-by date. It's May, and she only bought it as a Christmas gift to herself last November. The bint paid nearly eighteen hundred quid for it. Both of them are running down the street with their phones out in front of them. Phone-fronting. It's a craze. They are always phone-fronting, but tonight their trance-like-state is much deeper than usual. I think it's the morbid factor. The morbid factor is a bit like the X-factor. Hang on, I think they're the same thing. If there was a show called the morbid factor, the dead bodies would probably have more character and charisma than most of Cowell's future has-beens. Where was I? Oh yeah. Those two are steaming down the main street at a gallop. Oslo sports a contorted mincer's waddle at the best of times, but his little feet are going ten to the dozen tonight, and it's making him look like Stewie Griffin on speed. Cheryl's not much better. Both of them have their heads down and eyes glued to their phones in the hope of catching titbits about the bombing before they get to the scene. One of the most amazing things about their phone-fronting antics, which is a common theme among their type, is their ability to be transfixed to their phones while walking at running speed, and not bumping into anything or anybody, and not getting run over by one of those soundless electric cars. Apparently, those low-noise emitting vehicles are listed as one of the top ten most dangerous consumer products on the market today. It's not because you can't hear them shooshing down the street at you while you're trying to cross it. It's because if you own one, you're likely to get slapped around the back of the head for turning into one of those annoying environmentalist types who rams their recycling values and ethics down everyone else's throats. Then, they overstuff their blue wheelie bins for self-dispensed brownie points and spout shite about global warming and melting ice caps. They're missing the fact that they've just bought a twenty-five-thousand-pound car that was produced by a monstrous fossil-fuel-guzzling car plant in some politically corrupt third world country with no policies or regulatory standards on pollution. If they were that environmentally conscientious, they would have bought a fucking bike or a horse and cart. I don't know what's got into me? I'm a tad more testy than usual. I think it's these straps that have me pinned down in this bag. I can't get near my nads for a bit of rough-tongued self-soothing. The royal couple are on a mission, and there's no getting between those two when there's gossip to get. Especially the kind of juicy fodder that follows a supposed terrorist bombing. We've just been stopped by the police cordon. It's three miles away from the bomb site. It's busy. There must be over a thousand people here. It's a mixed crowd. Some are obviously worried about loved ones because they can't contact them. So, they're frantically redialling and texting, and in-boxing, and Facetiming, and Snapchatting, and Whatsapping, and E-mailing, and Skyping, and Instagramming. Cheryl and Oslo have suddenly become aficionados and the fount of all knowledge on terrorism, counter-terrorism tactics, immigration and border control. They've got nine-hundred-and-ninety-eight people on hand who are primed to listen to their twaddle because they're all the same. Everyone at the scene, and across the country, and across capitalist society, knows who bombed who and why. They're all swollen-up with knowing, and just bursting at the seams to let each other know that they know.

A bomb went off, and people have been injured and killed. It seems as if everyone wants a piece of it, in one way or another.

A bomb went off, and people have been injured and killed. For someone, the life of their loved one has ended in the most tragic and unfair circumstances. They don't care how it happened or who was responsible. Not yet. They only know that their heart has broken.

Undeterred by the actuality of a bombing that had just claimed the lives of people who were just going about their daily business. And, by the presence of a thousand others, who were worrying, grieving and speculating. And, by the idea that politicians were scheming and calculating on how the event could be used to their advantage, Chez and Oslo did what was expected of them. They started a Facebook page and a crowdfunding page to raise money and awareness to support anyone affected by the blast. The likes and pounds poured in. They were proud of that.

Kevin

I'm engaged in an activity that most people would call recovering from chronic drug addiction. Well, at least I think that's what I'm doing. I've been in rehab for six-and-a-half weeks now, and everyone in here keeps talking about "recovery." Recovery this, recovery that, recovery for breakfast, dinner and tea. The ex-junkies are queuing up to tell me that they're "in recovery now," and their claim to fame lies in the number of days clean they have achieved. They don't want to entertain the title, ex-junkie. I wonder why? There's one guy who tells me twice in every three hours how many days clean he is. He's up to ten days so far and counting. I keep telling him that I know already because he told me earlier. But it doesn't register. I'm not alone though. He tells everyone. I think his entire day comprises of constantly circulating the rehab and telling everyone how many days clean he is. He's starting to get right on my tits. There are thirty-three other happy campers in this joint, and seven staff. They're starting to get right on my tits too. Tits too. Tits too. If I said that three times quickly, I'd sound like an owl. On my second day, when I came around in the old doc's office, I refused the detox medication he offered me. Something strange happened. I thought that I had passed out. Not so, say some. The doc and the staff team claim that I had a kind of cathartic, spiritual experience. I don't know about that one. Sounds suspect, at best. At the time, I was convinced that my grandfather was in the room with me, and he was comforting me by stroking my head. Now I'm not so sure. It might have been the old doc. Probably was. The memory is fading and even though I want to, I can't retrieve it. When I refused the detox medication, I half-pretended that I was going cold turkey just to prove that I could, and to wind everyone else up, Sick Boy from Trainspotting did the same thing. My hero. On the other side of my kidology, something changed during my blackout, or whatever it was. It's hard to explain, mainly because I don't understand it. I seem to have had enough of that life.

"Nonsense sonny boy…… we're just having a wee bit of a break………. bit of R. 'n.R… you know it makes sense………. Won't be too long now though……… couple of weeks and we'll be back in the saddle……… yeeeehaaarrrrr……… cowboy……. can't wait… you and me both know that the drugs are much better when you lay off them for a bit………. makes sense here, sonny boy ………… can't deny it………… you really can't……. and anyway…………… might be a chance of a ride while were in here……………. the skanks here are rough though………. junkie birds… all gummy and baldy-mouthed ………… and slack-fannied……… after too many years on the gear and the game… ……..to be sure … to be sure……………… but me 'n you sonny boy… bit of shagging practice…………. yeeeehaaarrrr, cowboy … ride 'em high… ride 'em rough… that's what we always say……………. !"

Coming off the methadone and the dolly-mix-up of other drugs in the first two weeks was as rough as fuck. The shitting and barfing subsided after the first week and a bit. When the wave of physical symptoms subsided, the psychological assault kicked in. I'm not sure what's worse. The physical withdrawals are just that. They are simple enough to understand, but still hard to accept. It's a different ball game altogether when the head veers west. I have enough trouble as it is with the torturous goings-on in my cranial dungeon. The drugs usually keep that noise at bay. Partly, that's the point of taking them. There's peace in them-there hills, from time to time. From other time to times, such as drug-droughts or cash-quandaries, the noise levels go straight back up. This makes me think. The dudes who run this rehab tell me they have tons of experience with this addiction and this recovery malarkey. Yet, the reason I took drugs, apart from the fact that they're really juicy, is because my life was intolerable without them. I wonder how they reconcile themselves with those two opposing perspectives. Drug addiction made my experience of living tolerable. That's to say, that being a drug addict was less painful that not being one. Now, I need to learn how to tolerate living without drugs. So, what am I really recovering from? The drug addiction? Or on the other hand, an intolerable life? Jeez. I've just spangled my own noggin. I'll wait for a few more weeks until I get my bearings and the lay of the land, then I'll ask that Mike fella about it. Him and the rest of those other fuckers don't seem trustworthy.

"Tellin yi Sonny boy ………………………..Listen to me !"

Tilly

Her face epitomised gentleness. She was totally innocent and fragile, and she made no effort to hide it. In the house where she was born, she sat on the second stair from the bottom. The stair carpet was a deep red, clean and comfortable. She loved that red carpet, In fact, she loved the whole house. Every part of it. To the unobservant eye, she looked lost and alone and unsure of her place in this world. She entered this mood often. Quietness and stillness seemed to suit her. Her demeanour, when she was like this, was an unsettling thing to witness. It could leave the casual observer wondering if there was something deeply wrong with her. Had she been hurt in some way? Had something happened, and was she too afraid to tell anyone about it? Could she be depressed? Was she traumatised? Or, was she just seeking attention? She could leave you feeling helpless because when asked if she was OK, she was almost unresponsive. Could she be temporarily catatonic? Could this be a fugue state? Why is her response so limited?

At the top of stairs Natalie was cleaning the bathroom, and her husband Chad was a target for one of Jack's excursions. Jack ran, jumped and wrapped himself around his dad's leg while he was trying to negotiate a business deal on the phone. Chad was working from home for a day. Chad covered the phone's mouthpiece with his hand, and said: "if you don't get off my leg, you little tearaway, I will go down into the garage and let the tyres down on your bike." Jack was too young to really understand what his dad had said, but he roared with laughter anyway and shook his big head of black curly hair from side to side while tightening his grip. His dad walked around the room with his son sitting on his foot, pretending to be a boot.

Chad thought of calling him a Jack-boot, but then he thought better of it. Chad had no problem holding his composure with his new client during the important business. You could be fooled into thinking that he wasn't taking much notice of his little son, but that would be a mistake. Chad, like Natalie, was able to give his boy the attention he needed while he was engaged in another activity. He would never tell Jack that he was too busy, or that daddy had something more important to attend to. Jack knew that his dad was doing something else, but he never felt put aside or dismissed in any way. He also knew not to push his luck too far either, because his dad knew how to set healthy boundaries. He was content to swing about on his dad's leg for a bit while he got on with his phone call. A moment later, he let go and rolled off in search of another adventure.

All of a sudden, Natalie stopped what she was doing, lifted her head, and cocked her ears. For a brief moment, she resembled an attentive deer, listening and looking for any untoward sounds or movement. "Ahhhhhh,", she noised, when she realised what was going on. "Tilly needs some loving," she said. Natalie wasn't talking to anyone. She was just expressing what she knew. She put down her cleaning tools and headed straight down to the second stair, to meet her nine-year-old daughter's needs. Natalie knew exactly why Tilly was sullen and sitting quietly on her own. She knew that her daughter was sometimes introverted. That this was part of her natural makeup; her innate character. But she also knew that most of the people in Tilly's world didn't understand introversion and timidity, and they didn't want to. They automatically judged and condemned it. Or, they believed they were being kind and concerned by trying to rescue Tilly from her experience. But really, they were just trying to alleviate their own discomfort. Most of the people in Tilly's world, apart from those closest to her, adored and idolised success and its champions. Not shyness. They admired the brash and outlandish characteristics that are normally associated with celebrity-ism. The selfie-obsessed. Tilly was, and always would be, the exact opposite and she had no desire to be anything or anyone else. Natalie knew all of this. So, she stood in front of her daughter and said nothing. Instinctively, Tilly stood up and wrapped her arms around her mother neck. Then she jumped up and wrapped her long, lanky, nine-year-old legs around her waist. Her mother held her tight and walked around the house while her daughter clung to her front. Natalie went to the fridge and told Tilly to choose anything she wanted. She told her daughter that she could have fizzy pop, jelly, chocolate and ice cream all mixed together if she wanted it. She knew that Tilly would refuse because she wanted comfort food. Not treats. Instead, Tilly asked her mother to make her a plain egg sandwich with tomato ketchup and a glass of cold milk. This was one of her favourite snacks. "Of course I will honey. Let's do it together" said Natalie. Soon afterwards, Tilly went off and found a colouring book. Fort the next two hours, she sat quietly in her favourite corner of the big sitting room. Occasionally, Jack bounced by. Literally. Every time he passed, she raised her eyes and gave him a soft, warm smile.

Kevin's dream

I'm engaged in an activity that most people would call, wondering what the fuck happened during the dream I had last night. Yesterday, I attended my first counselling session with Mike. He told me that he had left me to get through my detox because it takes about six weeks or so before all the residual effects of the drugs leave the body. He said there wasn't much point in counselling before that happened. He started by saying that the first few sessions would give us a chance to get to know each other a bit better. Then, he briefly explained the therapeutic programme that I would need to go through, to keep the courts happy. Well, he didn't say that directly but I got the feeling that if I fucked about, then my court report would say so. And Mr Lispy Wig was waiting in the wings for my return. I don't think he's going to forget about me for a while. Let's hope our paths never cross again. For my sake.

"Fuck 'im sonny boy... Fuuuuckkkkk immmmmm!"

Mike said that we work the twelve-step programmes of Narcotics and Alcoholics Anonymous at the rehab. He overemphasised the WE part. Maybe he thinks I'm in his gang. He, and it, all sounded a bit mumbo-jumbo-ish to me. I didn't take much notice of either. Just to get me started, as Mike put it, he said that I should think about writing my life story. He told me that the written work would form the basis of our counselling sessions. I told him that I didn't know where to start. He looked at me while he rubbed his bristly chin with left hand; as if he was in deep thought. Then he said, quite simply, "just start with the first thing you remember when you were a child." I don't think he needed to act and look as if he was considering his response. It felt and sounded like an old script. I didn't say anything.

"Yeah... but that's you all over nowadays... Sonny boy... letting these fuckers take the piss... where's your head at? ...... for fuck's sake... give your napper a rattle... c'mon man... the past is the past is the past is the past... past... past... passsssssssst..."

It played on my mind all day. The very first thing I could remember as a child? I must have repeated that question to myself over one hundred and seventeen times until I fell asleep. That's when I dreamt the dream. Obviously.

Everything was dark. Black dark. As with all dreams, I was at the centre of it. I knew I was there; that I existed, but not in relation to anything or anyone else. After all, we need other people and things to know that we exist. However, I wasn't alone or lonely. There was just me, and the darkness that I occupied. No, that's not right. There was no distinction between me and the darkness. They, or we, were the same thing. It wasn't a threatening or foreboding darkness. It was just dark. I wasn't afraid or worried in any way, and I didn't have any questions about my situation. I didn't know if I occupied a body or not, and this didn't concern me either. In fact, the idea of questioning the whole situation never arose. Nothing did. I was just there, so to speak. But "there" was not a particular place. It wasn't like outer space or a vacuum of some sort, not that I've ever been in either of those places. It was just me as the darkness, and the darkness as me. I don't even know if it was darkness. That's the only word I have to describe it. It wasn't cold, and it wasn't hot. There were no smells or tastes, or sensations of any kind at all. I didn't have sight, touch, smell or any other senses or experiences. That's no totally true. There were sensations, but none that were familiar to me, in the traditional way. When I say there were sensations, I mean that I was the sensations. There was, or I was, a feeling of pure mass and density. Don't ask me how I knew this, I just did. It doesn't make sense to me either. The mass and density were one-thing, and it was huge, yet size-less, if there is such a word. It wasn't pleasant, and it wasn't unpleasant. The notion of time didn't come into play, but it wasn't timeless either. Although the whole thing was size-less and boundary-less, there was a form of movement. But, that movement was directionless. That's a real word. Directionless. I like that word. It wasn't up, down, left, right or sideways, and it didn't expand or contract. It, or I, just moved.

Then I woke up.

"Sonny boy!... Listen to me... listen closely.. whatever you do……………….you need to stay away from that stuff………………. it won't help……………. forget about it... just me and you..... eh Sonny boy ?"

Brutus, Cheryl and Eileen

What's that smell?

I don't believe my luck. Cheryl and that twat-of-a-mother of hers are taking me on a day out. This is gonna be brilliant fun. I can't wait. Cheryl and Olo were on a night out recently, when they heard a wolf whistle from across the street. When they looked over their shoulders, a drunk guy actually shouted at Cheryl "ahhhhhh, fat arse. Made you look." I agree. She looks as if she's trying to hide a mini space hopper down the back of her skin-tight leggings. As usual, Oslo dived to her rescue to stop her from finding out the truth about the actual size of her bum. He told her that, "people are just jealous because she looks just like Kim Kardashian." There are rumours going about that she's been nicknamed Kim's Car's Crashed Again. They've told everyone that they're going to Fat Fighters because those they've just announced that they've launched their "all new and improved dieting programme". The truth is, Cheryl is going because the jibes about her fat arse are becoming far too frequent. Eileen said she would go along to support her but really, she is going just to make all the fat people feel worse about themselves than they do already. And, to make sure that Cheryl doesn't lose too much weight, of course. Eileen needs Cheryl right where she is. Going on eleven stone, or thereabouts. She can't be letting her get ahead of herself by actually succeeding and perhaps losing a few pounds. After all, she might build some self-esteem or gain a little confidence. That won't do. Eileen has her persona to protect and she needs someone beneath her at all times, just in case it needs to be propped up. Like so many other mothers' daughters, this is Cheryl's lot in life. Oslo wanted to come along, but he had no chance. Eileen barred him from going out with her and Cheryl, for life. One time, he thought that he had a licence to be bitchy –gay and poker-straight-forward with Eileen, just because she was Cheryl's mother. Well, that's not true. Oslo believes that he has a licence to bitchy-gay and quick-cutting with anyone he likes. Apparently, as he sees it, "being gay makes it OK". That's one of his mantras. As far as I'm concerned, it's fucking cruel to talk to anyone like that, and it speaks to who you really are. When they were all out shopping together, Eileen popped into the changing room to try on a dress. She let her audience know that she was ready to go, then she swooshed out from behind the curtain like a contestant on Stars in Their Eyes. Cheryl knew the drill, so she applauded like a battery-operated cymbal-crashing monkey and giggled with delight before bestowing accolades at her mother's feet. Oslo's response was a bit different. He put his left hand on his hip and placed his right index finger on his lips, just as he was pouting them. Cheryl knew what was coming and tried to stop him, but it was too late. "Wellll...mmmmm...it's just not your colour, Eileen, and it does put a few pounds on those hips darling...not that I'm being critical you know...and I'm sure you'd want an honest opinion from someone with such good dress sense...much like yourself...don't you agree, Chez?" I must admit, even I ducked into the darkness of the handbag when he said it. Cheryl just pulled her hands up over her ears and buried her head in her lap. If she was on a flight back from Ibiza, you'd think she had just adopted the brace position. Eileen's response didn't match expectations. She just smiled and calmly said "Thanks, Oslo". That was it. She didn't even cut the shopping trip short or make excuses to go. She just carried on as if nothing had happened. When Oslo left, I expected Cheryl to get it in the neck. She didn't. All

Eileen said was, "Cheryl. Oslo won't be allowed to come shopping, or anywhere else, with us again". Then her facial expression changed in a way that Cheryl had never seen before, and her tone of voice dropped an octave or two, before posing the question, "RIGHT?" Cheryl said nothing. Ever so slightly, she just dropped her forehead forward and looked at the ground. She fell deathly silent. They both know that the message had been given and received. Nothing more was ever said about it.

Later, Cheryl told Oslo that she would end their relationship if he ever did or said anything like that again. She was serious. And he knew it. Nothing more was ever said about it.

Eileen's weight is tiptop. In fact, she looks like a million dollars when she's done up, and she knows it. She resembles one of those well-to-do, upper middle class, nearly middle-aged, very sexy newsreader types. I think they're called Milfy Money Mummies. It has to be said, she carries it well. For a twat , that is. We've arrived at the venue. Eileen is all decked out in a figure-hugging, cobalt-blue Dior dress, crowned with a Vivienne Westwood pearl and diamond-encrusted necklace. She's wearing her shiny black Prada high heels. She chose the ones with the red soles, as they will help her clickety-click all the way up to the podium for the weigh-in. She can't wait. Tonight Matthew, Eileen is going to be the slimmer of the year. Yayyyyy. She is first in the queue to take the stand, and she intends to make the audience seethe with envy by constructing and delivering a big fat lie. She introduces herself and tells everyone that she only needed to lose four pounds and she achieved her goal in only three weeks, and it was all because of the brand new Fat Fighter's programme. During her show, she subtly and seductively runs her hands up down her shapely, blue outline, and watches all the fatties bloat with rage as they compare themselves to her. She knows that what they see is totally unrealistic and unachievable in the short time they have left on the planet. She also knows that they will comfort-eat, or gorge on Greggs' finest delights as soon as they leave the building. And, that they'll go home feeling incredibly guilty but not know why. So, they'll open a couple of bottles of white wine in the name of unwinding and relaxation after a hard day of whatever they were doing. Then, half pissed, they'll slump into the sofa in front of the telly and tell themselves, "at least I lost three pounds this week, so a little pint or two of wine won't do much harm. And anyway, there are six more days to go before the next session. I'll make up for it by being extra good all week." As far as Eileen's concerned, it's mission accomplished. However, an unexpected Brucie bonus is about to fall in her lap. The Fat Fighters host went cock-a-hoop over herself when Eileen took centre stage and put on the show. She thought she had found a perfect poster girl for the new programme. Eileen's performance was pure gold, as far as the host was concerned. She approached Eileen and introduced herself in a manner that suggested they were old friends who hadn't seen each there for a few years. "Eileeeeen" the host sang, all opened-armed and welcoming-like. "I must say you are looking fabulous. Well done on your success. And SO quick, too! Have you been attending the Fat Fighters programme on the other side of town? I haven't had the pleasure of seeing you at our little gathering." Tonight, Eileen was only borderline sociopathic, but she could still smell contemptuous manipulators at a thousand yards. After all, she was Queen in that kingdom. She decided to play along for a little bit because delivering the coupe de grâce too quickly wasn't much fun.

The entertainment value shot up considerably when the intended victim's sense of security was high. Especially when her victim was responsible for elevating it herself. Let the games begin, thought Eileen. "Oh thanks, Joyce. What a nice thing to say. It is Joyce, isn't it? I am sure we have met somewhere before. I just can't place it. I think it might have been at the Lord Mayor's reception last October. I was lucky enough to be invited by a friend, you know. I don't usually attend such prestigious events. I'm sure you're more accustomed to things like that though"

Joyce was a player. "Well Eileen, thank you, thank you. I think we might have passed each other on the stairs that evening" she lied.

"I think you might be right Joyce"

Joyce posed her next question, with the familiarity of a family member. "Eileen, I wonder if you would be interested in attending our event on a more regular basis? In fact, I am looking for someone to help me co-host the delivery of our new programme. Is this something you might be interested in?"

Eileen feigned her response, to disguise its patronising nature. "Oh, Joyce! What a lovely thing to say. To consider me, of all people, to help you with such a thing. To be able to help people to change in such a meaningful way. I'd love to help. Thank you so, so much."

"Well Eileen, I think we would make such a good team. I just can't wait to get started. This is so exciting. I love my job. And I'm sure you'll love it too. So glad to have you on board. So glad."

"Me too Joyce. Me too. Mmmmm…just one little thing though, Joyce?"

"Anything Eileen. Anything. How can I help?"

"Well...I just need to get something clear in my head first, Joyce"

"Yes, Eileen. What's that?"

"Well, …we are going to be promoting and hosting the NEW Fat Fighters programme. Yes?"

"Ehhh…Yes, Eileen. Of course"

"Well…Joycey"

Joyce did not like that. She did not like being called Joycey. And Eileen's tone tasted a little sarcastic. Maybe she imagined it, she thought. Let it go. Eileen's contribution to the new programme would be well worth it. Maybe it's me. It's been a busy night. I'm tired, she thought. "Ehhh…..Yes. E…Eileen," stammered Joyce. She hadn't stammered since junior school. "What the…."

"Can you tell me what was wrong with the old Fat Fighters programme, Joycey? Was it not working properly? Why did you change it?"

She fucking called me Joycey again, Joyce thought. Followed by the realisation that she had just swore to herself for the first time since her divorce, over thirteen years ago. Fuck. She thought. Followed by, Fuck, I've done it again. Fuck. She wasn't having this. She has lost seven stone in three years. She was down to just over fourteen stone, and damn proud of it. She wasn't taking this shit from anyone. She needed to raise her game, and her voice. "Excuse meeee, Eileen dear. I don't quite understand what you mean by that."

"Ooooh" Eileen mouthed, just under her breath. "Fish on. And it's a big one"

"Excuse meeeeeee," shrieked Joycey.

"Oh, nothing DEAR" Eileen stamped. "Let me explain. It's quite simple, so I'm sure someone like YOU will be able to understand it. You see, I'm asking why you've decided to change the programme and come up with a new one. Really Joycey, there must be a reasonable explanation for this. After all, you lot have been running the same old show for the past forty years, and now you've decided it needs to change? You're ever so keen to tell the world that you've changed it, but you haven't said why you changed it. It's a simple enough question."

Joyce was game, she thought. She was up for the battle. So in she went: "Yes, and it's a simple enough answer. I'm sure someone like YOU will be able to understand it, Eileen"

Oh goody goody gumdrops, the big fish is a fighter, thought Eileen. She watched Joyce's nervous reaction, as a wicked smirk spread across her own mouth. This told her that her foe was all blubber and bluster. She knew this anyway, and her predatory eyes narrowed and zoomed in on their target.

Joyce continued: "The programme was changed to improve it, Eileen. Nothing's perfect, you know. In my opinion, I think the owners were being humble and modest in admitting that the programme could be improved." She was pleased with herself and her response. She believed she had her opponent on the ropes with her counter-punch. She straightened her back a little and rolled her shoulders back to show her defiance.

Eileen paused for a few seconds, just to heighten Joyce's sense of security before she kicked her off her perch. Then she said: "Joyce, dear, you and I both know that the old Fat Fighters programme told people that they can and should control what they eat and drink. So, what is it saying now, with its new programme?"

Joyce's shoulders fell a bit, and her slouch resurfaced. Eileen noticed it, and she wasn't about to miss the opportunity, so she upped the ante. "Look Joycey, the facts are the facts, and they speak for themselves. Historically, Fat Fighters and all of those other chubby-chum parties are the same. They're all designed to make sure that you don't lose weight, and if you do, they make sure that you will put it back on again and come running back with your weekly subscription fee. If they were too successful, they would be out of business within a few years. Wouldn't they? I mean, look at you. How long have you been at it now? I bet you've been coming here for more than five years. That's the average, you know. For others, like you, it's much, much longer. The statistics don't lie. You know that the overall success rate is less than ten percent. So tell me, Joyce, what other business do you know of that flourishes with a ten percent success rate? Is that why you're changing the programme? Because you and your leaders know that it's not working. That it's losing its dedicated followers, because most are old and dying from obesity-related health problems, and the new breed of younger fatties aren't interested in the old fuddy-duddy Fat Fighters anymore? Is that it Joycey? Is it not as fashionable as it used to be? How much do you weigh now, after all the years you've been coming?"

Joyce tried to think of a response, but she was battered and her head spun. She stammered again, only worse this time, "Eh…L…L…L… Listen E…E…Eileen"

Eileen came back hard and quick. She leaned into Joyce's face with a stiff, neatly manicured nail situated at the end of her white bony index finger, and scowled at Joyce in a hissing whisper: "NO…You fucking listen…M…M…Missy F…F…F…Fatty P…P…Pants. If you and your pathetic fucking company wanted to help people to lose weight, you would tell them the fucking truth. But you don't. You manipulate them into believing that they have a problem with food and drink when they don't.

Two questions appeared in Joyce's mind. They first was, "Is this Hannibal Lector's Wife?" and the second, "I wonder if she eats liver and Fava beans?" She almost coughed up a laugh, but it stuck in her throat because it couldn't get past the ball of fear that had taken up residence there. She heard herself gulp, repeatedly.

Eileen pressed on. "You keep your cash-paying customers coming back, week after week, by leading them on. You convince them they'll get *there* eventually, by colluding with their gluttonous behaviour. And in turn, as a host, you get to do the same. Don't you? You tell them that it's OK to pig-out every now and then, just as long as they don't give up and keep coming back. You tell them that it's OK to eat this, and it's not OK to eat that. And worst of all, you have the audacity to tell them when they are permitted to SIN. Who are you people? The fucking Borgias? Tell them the truth! Oh, but you won't, will you? And you won't tell them the truth for two reasons, Joycey. Do you know what those reasons are? Do you? They're really very, very simple, Joycey. Firstly, if you told the truth, then you and your scabby business would implode within months. Secondly, just like you Joycey, the people who attend these pathetic events don't want to hear the truth. In fact, that's the last thing any of you want to hear. Isn't that right, Joycey?"

Joyce became a vortex. Everything in her spun in ever-decreasing and downward spirals. She was sure that she was going to pass out. But she was transfixed, she had no option, she had to listen-on.

"And what is this truth, Joycey? Eh? Do you know? Is it lurking somewhere in the background, but you're too shitty to face it? Is that it Joycey, dear? Is that why you keep this puny group going? So that you can hide together, and disguise your fatness and greed? Is it? Of course it is. So........ let me be the first to introduce you to the truth, Joycey. Then you can tell all your plumpy pals about it and perhaps, for once, you could do some of them a favour."

Joyce thought, NO!

Eileen's gun was loaded and pointed. And she wasn't about to relinquish pulling the trigger. No Sireeee Bob. She fired. "The thing is Joycey, you and your kind don't have a problem or an unhealthy relationship with food. In fact, it's impossible to have a relationship with food at all. Food is inanimate. It can't answer back. The truth is, you don't know how to have a relationship with hunger. That's all there is to it. It's got nothing to do with the food you eat or don't eat. It seems, that for you lot, feeling hungry is utterly intolerable. Try standing on the podium and announcing that, Joycey."

Eileen continued, but this time she didn't attempt to hide her derision. In fact, she put on her best mocking voice and pretended to be Joyce. She said, " Good afternoon ladies, and any stray gentlemen that have wandered in. As you know, this is the new Fat Fighters programme. The old one died because it was shit. Today we're not going to try controlling what we eat or drink because we're going to learn how to be hungry. Sound good? It only takes one day to learn and once you've mastered it, you'll never need to come back here again. So, from now on, we're not going to talk about food or what we can and cannot eat or drink. In fact, we're never going to talk about it again. So, who's first?"

Joyce didn't expect this. She didn't know what to expect. But she didn't expect this. She tried to talk. To respond. Anything would have done, but she was totally dumbstruck. Then, the dam burst. As soon as the wailing started, Eileen clicked her shiny Pradas in the style of Dorothy from the Wizard of Oz, then spun on her pointy heels and cat-walked off down the hall with her middle finger raised in the air for her audience behind her. All she had to say, was "see ya, fatties!"

I thought I was coming out for a good laugh at the humans behaving ridiculously about food. This turnout couldn't have been more unexpected. It doesn't happen often, but I'm speechless. I've never seen a performance like that in my life. Eileen is a cruel fucker, no doubt about it. Cheryl's bubbling her eyes out. Again. All she wanted was a couple of inches off the circumference of her bum. She's tagging along behind her mother, feeling humiliated. Again. It's unusual, but I feel sorry for Cheryl. A bit.

Just to rub salt in the wound, Eileen said "You should have

brought Oslo along tonight, Cheryl. He would have loved it"

Thank fuck I'm a dog.

Natalie and Chad

"Natalie?"

"What hun?"

"Believe it or not, I was talking to one of the lads the other day about unconditional love. Do you think there is such a thing?"

"I think it depends. What do you mean?"

"You know. You've heard of it before. Don't be a dick,Nat. This is hard enough to talk about as it is. Unconditional love. What do you think about it?"

"I'm not being a dick, hun. I'm being serious. I think it depends on what you mean. I don't know if the phrase makes any sense?"

"What do you mean? Now I sound like a dick? What do you mean about it not making any sense? I don't understand."

"Well, think about me and you. We love each other. Right?

"Right"

"Does that mean that I will love you unconditionally, even if you are mean to me? If so, then that's not love. Is it? That's something else. Or, does it mean that there are no conditions to our love. If that was the case, then that wouldn't be love either. That would be something else too. There are loads of conditions to our love for each other. We talked about them all the time, in the past. Remember? Fairness, for example. Our love for each is totally dependent on fairness. We agreed, a long time ago, that we would always let each other know where we are or where we are going, no matter what. We agreed that we would never cause any unnecessary worry that way because it would be unfair. Do you remember? We made a commitment of fairness to each other"

"Yes"

"So, one of the conditions of our love for each other is fairness. Another is safety. Do you remember that one?"

"Eh…oops…no?

"Ha ha. You doughnut. If I don't let you know where I am and it causes you to worry, then you need to able to get pissed off at me, if you need to, without me getting all defensive and retaliating. You or I need to feel safe to disagree with each other. Remember?"

"Of course I remember."

"Oh, yeah. You remember now, because I've just told you."

"Fuck off?"

"Look chad, if you and I looked back over the years at how our relationship and our love for each has developed, we would find loads of conditions to it. We're accustomed to them now, so we don't think about them. Until one of us breaks the conditions. Which is usually you."

"Twat"

"Ha ha. So our love is conditional then. Very!

"I guess it is. I never thought of it that way."

"Me neither hun. It's a good question though. The other thing is, what did you and your friend mean by the word love? Where you using the word in relation to love between a couple of adults?"

"Yes. Probably. I never thought about it at the time. Are you saying that there is more than one kind of love?"

"Yes. And no."

"Oh, here we go. Miss Ambiguity Conundrum has entered the building. Another thing. Anyone heard for Kevin lately?"

"No. The last time we heard, he was somewhere in the Netherlands. Why did you ask that?"

"I think of him from time to time. I always liked him."

"Me too. When you called me Miss Ambiguity Conundrum, it reminded of Eileen when she used to call me Little Miss Mary Martyrdom, because of my interests in the world and its people. She called Kevin lots of other names as well."

"Sorry to side-track you, Nat. I was asking whether you thought there was more than one type of love?"

"Look at it like this, Chad. We love each other, right?"

"Right"

"And we love our kids too, right?"

"Right"

"So, do you think that the love between adults and the love between adults and their children is the same?"

"Well…ehrr…yes…and no."

"Classic answer. Priceless."

"Yeah, yeah. You're so clever. You know what I mean. It is the same, but then again, it's not."

"Correct-amondo. You see what I mean. It's the same word, but it's used to say two different things. And guess what?"

"Oh, do surprise me"

"Our love for each other is conditional, yes?"

"Yes, yes and yes. We've established that. Do you need to go around the houses Nat?"

"No, but I like to. I like the scenery where we live."

"Oh lord, why did I marry this woman? Would you get on with it."

"OK. Our love is conditional, but the love from a parent to a child is unconditional. That's if the parent is capable of love, though. Ain't that great?

"Now you're making it all too complicated. Hang on, that means you're saying some parents are incapable or unable to love?"

"I'm not saying any of this is factual. It's just my way of looking at it."

"Yes. I know that. But you are saying some people aren't able to love and some are."

"I am indeed. Have you never met anyone who is unable to love?"

"I suppose Eileen fits the bill"

"I imagine she does. And I think it goes even further than that."

"Pray, do tell."

The love between adults is one thing and the love from adults to children is another, but what about love in all the other parts of life?

"Like what?"

"Like the love of nature, the love of football, the love of cakes. You know, the love of things and stuff."

"That's not real love though"

"Really? Then why do people say it then?"

"It's probably because that's how they feel about it. I suppose?"

"You see. There's another example of people using the word love when they probably mean something else. And I'll tell you what, I think it goes even further again."

"I'm all ears."

"We've spoken about love in relation to someone or something else, yes?"

"I concur, captain"

"Well, what about love on its own?

"What about it?"

"Do you know what I mean?"

"I'm not risking it. Tell me"

"I'm talking about the feeling of love when it arrives on its own for no apparent reason. Like when you're standing at a bus stop, or in the queue at Aldi, and you get flooded by pure love just because you're a human being. That kind of love".

"You're naive Nat".

"You think?"

"I don't think, I know. I think the love you're talking about is rare. I don't think a lot of people experience life the way you do."

"No?"

"No, Nat. I love you, you know."

"What do you mean."

"Dick!"

IS THIS TRUE

Kevin and Mike

I had my second counselling session with Mike yesterday. He asked me how my life story was coming along. I told him that I hadn't started it yet, but I kept quiet about the dream. To be honest, I felt a bit embarrassed about it. Feeling embarrassed is new. In the recent and not so recent past, I refused to feel anything. Partly, that was the point of taking so many drugs. To control, or avoid how I felt. There's a down-side to that strategy. The good feelings, like happiness and contentment go in the bin along with not-so-good ones. Mike didn't make a fuss about my complacency around the life story, but he did make a few notes in his little blue book. Probably meat for the court report. I needed to be careful. I've got no intention of returning to my former life. Fuck that. However, the crew at this place don't seem to be the accommodating types. Their house rules say it all. No swearing. For fuck's sake, I was brought up on swearing. When I was a kid, everyone swore. It was how we communicated. I'll put that in my life story. In fact, I'll include as many swear words as possible, just for flavour. Another rule is, no newspapers or magazines, or books of any kind. I am allowed to read, but only if it's Narcotics or Alcoholics Anonymous official literature. Nothing else. Another rule is, no inappropriate clothing. This means things like football shirts, t-shirts with slogans, camouflage patterns or anything that might be sexually suggestive. And no hats, sunglasses or scarves. The residents police all the rules. Every two weeks, a different resident is nominated as the enforcer of the rules, and he or she is issued with a notebook. The nominee writes down the offender's name and reports to the staff. Every infringement carries a penalty. A fine of fifty pence, up to a maximum tally of five pounds per week. This is deducted from the weekly allowance, which is usually paid by the State through unemployment benefits. Apparently, these rules and penalties are in place to help formerly drug and alcohol addicted people to change their behaviour because it's supposed to teach them to have respect for societal values and boundaries. The rationale behind the rules and penalties is, that addicted people are innately selfish, inconsiderate and dishonest. It seems that most of us do what we like when they like and fuck the consequences to all concerned. This is Mike's take on it. It's a dubious justification. He's insisted that addiction is a three-fold disease. A mental, physical and spiritual malady, as he put it. He reckons that people who suffer from it and want to recover from it, need to build strong morals and values or they will fail.

"Sonny boy!.....................What's the story?..............why are you even considering any of this?................you know the dance ....you know the score............these cunts don't know what they're on about................let's go man.............we'e had enough of this shit............let's go..............!"

I asked Mike what he meant by that comment. Addition is a disease and learn to live with it? He's advised me to read the literature, as it speaks about the nature of the of addiction and that fact that it is incurable. He said, that anyone who has it can never be free of it, so they must learn to live with it for the rest of their lives. I wondered if he was taking the piss, but he looked deadly serious. He glared at me, all stern-like, and said, "You're living with a killer, and you will need to learn about it and come to terms with it, otherwise you will relapse into drug use again. Then you could end up in prison, or in an institution, or dead." I thought to myself, NAAAAHHHHHH, you can't be serious?

"That's what I was thinking Sonny Boy………………….naaaaaahhhhh!......same as……….were on the same page here………….me and you …………...naaahhhhhhhhhhh   they're brainwashers……….never heard so much shite in my life…………..a disease……………...as fuckin if…………....ask the cunt to prove it…………..where's his evidence ……..nahhhhhhhh me and u Sonny boy ……………....let's go …………c'mon man !"

"Mike. You're having me on. Really?" He must've seen the quizzical look on my face and it looked as if he felt the threat of my impending hysterics. He stiffened, and said "This is no joke Kevin. This is deadly." I knew that if I started wisecracking, it might mean foregoing the collection of two hundred pounds and a direct trip to the pokey without passing GO. So instead, I started a debate. Unbeknownst to my mate Mike, I read the two-booked library from cover to cover when I was withdrawing. What else was I going to do? Fifteen sleepless nights gave me ample time for it. As far as I was concerned, I was forearmed with lots of info for the up and coming discussion. I couldn't fuck about with him like the magistrate, though. Too risky. Apart from that, he seemed like a decent character. Lispy McSquint deserved it. Nasty little cretin, that one. Anyhow, off I went. "Can you tell me a bit more about this Mike. How is this disease of addiction contracted?" Mike was wise enough to know that I was baiting him. Instead of reprimanding me, he gently said "This isn't important right now, Kevin. All you need to know at this time, is that addiction is a debilitating illness. And the best way to deal with it, is by working through the twelve steps. Addicts and alcoholics think they know it all Kevin. I've been in recovery for twenty-six years, and I've seen and heard it all. A little humility is all that's needed to get you on your way. Do you think you could do that? After all, you've not made a very good job at running your own life so far. Have you? Maybe you should let someone with more experience help you for a while?" He had a point. Maybe I should? Instead of acting like a knob, my default setting, I respectfully replied "Mike, you have a point. Can I think about it?"

"Sonny boy ………… Sonny boy …………

Sonny boy …………

Sonny boy … Sonny boy ………… Think about it?….. Think about it?……………. What is there to think about?………… You know this tadger is talking shite…………… Just fuck im off and let's go………………… Listen to me…"

Again, Mike gently said "Of course Kevin. Most drug addicts and alcoholics are defiant rule breakers. They find it difficult to accept help. It's understandable that you feel and act the way you do. Now, would you like to tell me a little bit about your family life when you were growing up?"

"Why not. Can't see any harm in it" I heard myself saying.

"I can………….plenty of harm……….fukinnn…….Peeee lenty."

This was surprising. I don't usually allow myself to feel surprised. I don't like it. These things need to be drugged away, I thought. But no-can-do today, because of my new drug-free lifestyle. My next thought was, SHIT?

I dismissed my fears and began to talk to Mike. He's asked me about my immediate family members. Mother, father, siblings and pets. What were their names, and what types of characters were they? The pets thing threw me. I asked him "why pets?" "Because they're members of the family, and they're important," he said. Simple enough answer. Mike seems easy to like. That rhymes. Ha. Anyway, I start to begin to give him the low-down on the mob back at home.

"Well Mike." No sooner had I said it when a lump appeared in my throat. Not a physical lump. I wasn't trying to swallow a golf ball. It was one of those emotional lumps. I don't like those. They need to be drugged away, I thought. Then I thought, I think like that a lot.

"Are you OK Kevin?" asked Mike.

"Not really, Mike." I replied. "I feel upset at the idea of talking about my family." This didn't sound like me. Where was all the overly descriptive banter and the piss-taking?

"It's OK Kevin. This is normal for someone who has been using and abusing drugs for as long as you have. Anyone with your type of background would feel the same way."

"Thanks, Mike. I don't know what I want to say"

"Tell me about your mother"

"She's OK, really. She's had a really hard life, you know. I feel sorry for her. I've never done her any favours. I've always been trouble. Even as a little boy, probably aged three or four or something, I was a handful. Always getting into trouble and always needing attention in one way or another. I've always been disruptive and problematic."

IS THIS TRUE ?

"How do you know this, Kevin?"

"Because she told me. All the family know it. It's common knowledge. That's why I fuck off across the world, whenever I can. To let them have some peace. Sorry for the swearing Mike."

"It's OK Kevin. You can swear as much as you like in these sessions. Just not in the main house with the other residents."

"That's contradictory and double standards, Mike."

"Do you think you could just trust me on this Kevin? I could explain it, but we don't have much time right now. Could you let it go until later on?"

"Ok, Mike. Sorry. I get like that. As soon as I see a fault in something or someone, I pick at it like a dried scab. It's one of those things that I do. It caused lots arguments at home. My mother made fun of me about it. She'd put on a cowboy's voice and call me Picker Critical, the bad-est moaner in the Wild Wild West. The rest of the family would laugh. So would I. But I didn't really think it was funny. It just made me worse. I'd dig my heels in and eventually get angry. But then she'd make even more fun of me by saying to everyone that I had my spurs in the dirt. I know she was only joking, but it didn't feel like it."

"Are you sure she was joking, Kevin?"

"What do you mean by that? What are you trying to say…? Sorry, Mike. Fucking hell. What's wrong with me? You're sitting here giving me your time, trying to help me out, and I'm barking at you like a rabid dog."

"No wonder. Perhaps you have a lot to bark about?"

"Maybe, Mike. You know, that reminds me. I was off the drugs a few years back, so I went to see a doctor on my own. I told him that I thought I had anger problems, and asked if he could he help. All he did was give me a shitty little leaflet on anger management. The first thing it said was that I can control my anger, so I should take steps to calm myself down. I went fucking ballistic. I started shouting at him and fucked off. I kept the leaflet and had a read at it on the bus. Later on, I wondered about it. Anger management? Would trying to control or manage my anger not just make it worse?"

"Of course it would Kevin. You're right. That's really insightful. But, that's state sponsored medicine and medics for you. If they can't medicate it, they don't recognise it as a legitimate problem. I'm on the same page. What good is an anger management leaflet, if a person's anger is fully justified? What if they don't want to, or need to calm down? Who do you think came up with such a blatantly stupid idea? Don't you think that this is a recipe for widespread depression?"

"Yes. The leaflet pissed me off as soon as I read it. Two days later I was back on the gear."

"It's understandable Kevin. Anyone in your situation would have done the same. It pisses me off too. What is someone supposed to do with a poxy leaflet if they were raised by violent and abusive caregivers who hurt them when they were children, and they couldn't defend themselves at the time because they were was too small? And now, as adults, the time had come to do something about it. What are they supposed to do if they have every right to despise these people for the way they were treated? What if they have every right to feel their boiling hot rage and they need to know that their desire to retaliate is legitimate? What if they have the right to lay all of this at the feet of these monsters? And what is a young person supposed to do with his anger, if some idiot schoolteacher berates and ridicules him in front of his friends? What is he supposed to do if he is made to feel excruciatingly ashamed, but he can't defend himself against these cowardly bullies because of the power they are given to wield over him? And what are teenagers supposed to do when they are chided and shouted-down by adults when all they are trying to do is break free and find their way in the world, so that the can go out and build a life of their own? What are they supposed to do with their fury at the ignorance and pettiness of these adults who try to crush them, when life compels them to go the other way and set themselves free? And what are grown adults supposed to do when they're forced to bear the indignation of listening to the thieving and lying politicians and corporate giants as they spout pure nonsense about making their lives better and saving them from all the evil in the world? What are they supposed to do with their humiliation, as they're conned and corralled into meaningless jobs and expected to be grateful and rejoice at being given the privilege of just getting by every month, while their credit card bills and accompanying stress rises steadily in the murky background? And what are old people supposed to do with their fervour, when their children are up and gone, and they're left bewildered by how fast their lives had passed. What are they supposed to do now, as they stare into a bleak future? What are they supposed to do with their despair and anguish as retirement and pitiful state pension looms, and at the same time they're asked to applaud tycoons like the Facebook owners for publicly giving away £45 billion to offset his guilt for decimating or capacity for human connection? Surely they all have the right not to calm down? Surely they have the right to feel the full weight of their anger and express it? Perhaps the anger management leaflet should have said something like this: Are you angry? Good! No wonder. Let's see it, and let's hear about it! What do you think Kevin? Sound good?"

"Sounds about right Mike. Can't see it happening though"

"Yeah. Me neither. Tell me a bit more about your mother. Did she ever smack or hit you?"

"Only a couple of times. I deserved it though."

"Did you?"

"Did I what?"

"Deserve it?"

"Yes. I was disruptive. I was uncontrollable. I was stealing from shops. Bringing police to the door. Playing truant from school. All sorts of stuff."

"What age where you when she hit you?"

"About eleven or twelve"

"Did she ever hit you when you were younger?"

"Not that I can remember, but my father did"

"Did he?"

"Yes"

"What age were you?"

"Can't remember. I was young. Probably four or five"

"What did he hit you for?"

"Fighting with my sister"

"How old was she?"

"Five or six."

"Did he hit her too?"

"Yeah. Both of us"

"For fighting with each other?"

"Yes"

"How do you feel about that?"

"That's the way it was, I suppose. Don't think it did me any harm"

"No?"

"No"

"Would you include these things in your life story, to get you started? I'd love to read it with you."

"I'll try Mike."

"Good. Go get yourself a smoke and a cuppa and I'll catch you later on"

"Cheers Mike… eh… thanks."

"Well done Sonny boy ………………….now he knows about you…………how are we supposed to deal with

that…………he's like the rest of them…………he'll use it against you……………did Eileen not teach you anything……………you know what she says about letting people see your feelings…………………now there's no choice……………let's fucking go………………"

"I don't like this. I don't think this is the place for me."

Chad and Joe

Chad and Joe went mountain biking together, as often as possible. Chad was a downhill semi-pro back in the day, and he loved that his son was keen on the sport. At times, when they stopped for rest in the middle of the woods, when it was quiet and when no one else was about, they enjoyed a good conversation. This was one of those times.

"Dad"

"What son!"

"Where do ideas come from?"

"From your brain, son"

"Duh. Yeah. I know that, Dad. But what about ideas that weren't there before, and they suddenly just appear. New ideas. Not the ones that come from memory or experience. The ones that have never been in the brain before. Do you know what I mean?"

"Yes, son. That's' a good question. Let me think about it."

"OK"

Joe and Chas were quiet for a few minutes. They were comfortable in silence together.

Chas was first to speak. "Here's what I think about your question, son. I think ideas come from the place in you that is naturally creative. The thing about that though, is that I don't think that it can be proven. That's my take on it anyway. There are lots of theories about it, and people with great minds have pondered on the same question. Some of them have said that they know for sure and have even built theories around it. But in the end, I think it's one of those things that will always be a mystery. There are brilliant brain scientists who can show you which part of your brain lights up when you think creatively, but I think you are asking a question about something very different. I think it's similar to asking, where does a great singer's ability to sing come from? Geneticists might tell you that it's hereditary, and it may be, but I don't go for that. Or, it's like trying to explain why Lionel Messi is so good at football. Where does his creative ability come from? Do you know what I mean son? Are you following me?"

"Yes, dad. I know what you mean"

"I think it's a bit like insight. Being able to think of things and see things that other people can't. You know. Like, where does insight come from? Where does creativity come from? Where do ideas come from? I think they're, sort of, the same question. Or at least, they're all questions that are pointing to a similar thing. You know what I mean?"

"Sort of dad. It's making my head go a bit fuzzy"

"I know. It's enough to make anybody's head go fuzzy. I think it makes the head go fuzzy because it's such a mystery. If you think about it, a new idea, or intuition, or creativity, or whatever you want to call it, wasn't there a moment ago. And then, it is. All of a sudden, it just arrives. Don't you think that's amazing son?"

"Yes, dad. I do."

"You know what I really think about that question son?"

IS THIS TRUE ?

"No dad. What?"

"I think that all new ideas, and the other stuff, all come from the same place. I know that they arrive in the brain, but I don't think that they originate from there. I think that it's one of those things that make us human. Some animals that can do this, sort of. But not the way we humans can. I think it's all a bit mystical that stuff son. Lots of people will tell you that they know the answers to questions like this. And then they will tell you that they can help you to find out as well. But, you'd probably need to do what they say, or follow them, or something else. That's the other thing that makes us human, son. We are given new ideas, like special gifts, and we claim them as our own. As if we did it on purpose. As if it was a skill we had practised and mastered. No one can do this. No one can come up with new ideas at will, or when they want to. New ideas arrive when *they* want to, and not a moment sooner. Sometimes I wonder if we have the right to seize them and profit from them at the expense of others. That's where animals are different. "Anyway, son. Don't you think that it would be much better if it all just remained a mystery and that no one will ever really know?"

"Suppose so dad. But on the other hand, I think I would like to know the answer."

"There's a better question to ask yourself about stuff like this Joe."

"Is there, Dad? What?"

"You could ask yourself, why you want to know and what you would do if you found the answer?"

"That's the type of thing Mum would say."

"I know son. That's where I got it in the first place. You fit? Ready to go?"

"Yes, dad. Won't be long before I can thrash you, you know. Age is catching you up old man."

"Maybe, son. Not today though. Smell you at the bottom of the hill. Snooze you lose."

Brent and Eileen

They had planned to meet at the usual place, at the usual time. Brent was giddy with excitement because of Eileen's idea to break from the same old routine and see him on a Wednesday. Those words had him humming an obscure old tune from the early nineties, called "need a break from the old routine," by a band called Oui Three. Brent had a knack for remembering obscure one-hit wonders, along with masses of other useless information. He would have been hard to beat in a pub general knowledge quiz. Not that he would ever enter one. That would mean he would have to engage and socialise with other adults. Dicey. He might let his guard slip and risk the chance of being seen. Best to keep to himself. He did some socialising with others who were like him but that was always online, never in person. He knew it was much safer that way. With his considerable computer skills and code writing background, he could be whoever he wanted to be and disappear at the click of a mouse. He likened himself to Superman in that way. If he was feeling playful, he would recite superman's introduction and add on words of his own. "Brent McKenzie. Faster than a speeding bullet, more powerful than a locomotive, able to leap tall buildings in a single bound, and he can disappear with the click of a mouse." This made him titter and tee-hee to himself. Sometimes, he burst into full-on fits of laughter. He couldn't let it go too far though, because the overly tight skin around his face and lips would take on the appearance of an over-swelled cherry. If it went too far, he feared it would rupture. When this happened, it left him panting and gasping for air. He wasn't too bothered by the lack of air and his puffed-up circulatory system. In fact, in a sort of masochistic fashion, he actually drew some pleasure from the hysteria and physical discomfort. The thing that troubled him most about these episodes, was his lack of control. In the space within the few seconds between chuckling and bursting with laughter, he became momentarily lost and forgot himself. He didn't like this. It left him feeling vulnerable and exposed. He had a lot to hide. Although it was a fleeting feeling, it reminded him of what happens when he drank too much. He only ever drank too much once, and swore it would never happen again. One summer, he took himself to Ibiza for a break. He thought that a bit of sun would do him good. He booked into an all-inclusive holiday hotel because he intended staying put and relaxing by the pool for a week. On his first day, he decided to have a few drinks. He liked vodka and lemonade. Two or three at the most, never any more. He unpacked his bags and settled in by the pool watching, and ordered a drink. It was lunchtime and the temperature was in excess of thirty degrees. The heat made him thirsty, so he drank his first vodka a lot quicker than usual. The all-inclusive deal made it too easy for him to order another. Without realising it, he had ordered and drank six vodkas in quick succession. He didn't take account of the large continental alcohol measures, or the heat and dehydration. The next thing he knew, it was morning and he was being dragged out of bed and forcibly ushered from the hotel by two male Spanish staff members. They were hollering about something in Spanish. During his rousting, he could only make out two of their words. "Cámara and niños". That was all he needed to set him skittering off to the airport and jumping on the next available plane back home. During the flight, he experienced a few flashbacks of the previous day's events. He felt horrified. Not at his behaviour. He knew what he was and had no inclination to be otherwise. It was the idea that other people had seen him. Above everything else in his life, this is what haunted him the most. Eileen knew what he was to, and she didn't seem to mind it. In fact, on rare occasions, and Brent hoped tonight was one of them, she positively encouraged it. She didn't say or do anything in particular to support him. However, her silence and inactivity were all Brent needed to know that she didn't object. And in his world, Eileen's apathy was as good as permission. Sometimes, he wondered why Eileen colluded with him, but he could never quite figure it out. He tried not to think about it too much because every time he did, he always ended up panicking in case she ever used her knowledge to destroy him. It was true, that Eileen knew what he was, but Brent knew the same about her. He knew that she would put an end to him at the drop of a hat, and walk away feeling no more than if she had just swatted an irritating fly. In the same way as enjoying a little physical pain with his fits of laughter, he also enjoyed the risk of moving around the world with Eileen. He wondered if that's what she liked about him. The risk. The adventure. The taboo-ness of a mother associating herself with one of his kind. Did it thrill her in some way? He could only guess, because she would never tell him. The plain fact was that she had plenty of information to hang him with, yet he had nothing on her. He thought he did have something about three or four years ago, when she was being unusually chatty with him on one their nights out, after a few drinks. She seemed a lot looser than normal. They were discussing the act of murder, and how best to get away with it. Strangely enough, the topic of conversation wasn't that unusual for them. For once, Brent's ideas outshone Eileen's. Being fiercely competitive, Eileen came back with a semi-joke about her mother's death when she was a teenager. And how if anyone ever found out what really happened, then she could face historical manslaughter charges. As soon as she finished her sentence, Brent lit up with twinkling vengeance. He had something on her at last. He looked as if he had just struck gold. Eileen spotted it right away. She knew all about the sensation emitting from Brent, because she had lots of experience with it herself. Eileen was always on the lookout for the juicy fodder of other people's vulnerabilities. As soon as Brent noticed she had seen it in him, a surge of hot fear flushed up through him from the well in the pit of his lower abdomen. Instantly, his peculiar reddish complexion turned chalky white; his bottom jaw dropped slightly and he began to lift his arms. Then without saying anything, because he was dumbstruck, he stretched out his hands beseeching Eileen's forgiveness. With her next inhale, Eileen sobered up. Her spine straightened, her head lifted and her eyes narrowed like a bird of prey zooming in on its quarry. At the same time, her lips thinned and tightened. Brent knew what was coming. He'd been here once before and he didn't want to go back again. When they first met, he made a similar mistake. That one was much more trivial than this one though, so he knew that the imminent thrashing was going to be biblical, if not nuclear. Probably both. Unconsciously, his anus and teeth tightened in unison. Much like soldier at war, when he knows an inbound mortar bomb is heading straight for his foxhole. At the same time, he started making a low murmured "gnnnnnnnnnnnn" sounds, accompanied by distressed squeaky-mouse noises. To top it off, he was sure that he felt the first tiny drops of urine squirt from the end of his penis. Brent was a seasoned fantasist, if not a master on the subject. So, he did what all fantasists do when they feel feelings or experience thoughts they don't like. He dived for cover into one of his sub-personality-hero-types. All of a sudden, in a land far far away from Eileen, he became Dr Jones from Raiders of the Lost Ark, and the band struck up the accompanying theme tune. By the time he resurfaced to meet Eileen, she was gone. She had up-and-left, and he didn't notice a bit of it. He was relived and doubly worried at the same time. Relieved that he didn't need to face her, and worried that he would need to later on. When they next met, Eileen acted as if nothing had happened. She even seemed pleased to see him. Brent didn't care, he was just glad to have dodged a bullet. He wouldn't make the same mistake a third time.

As Brent waited for Eileen, he rested on a solitary bar stool facing the pub window into the high street. He thought about Eileen and her ability to instantly forget anything she'd said or done. It wasn't as if she was pretending to forget. It was as real as the early evening in front of him. She could move from mood to mood, thought to thought and action to action, seemingly consequence free. Especially when she was angry or spiteful. Which was almost all the time. He wondered if she had a conscience, or if she ever felt guilt or remorse. Then, he wondered if he was the same. Maybe that was it? Maybe it was their dire lack of concern for anyone else but themselves. Maybe this was why they were so good and bad together. As he sat there oscillating between pondering and fantasising, Eileen came swanning in through the pub's swinging doors sporting the mannerisms of a sheriff looking for a runaway, villainous cowboy. As usual, she looked stunning, and most of the men's heads turned when they saw her. Even in the later part of her fifties, she still oozed sex appeal and had a great figure with to-die-for dress sense. She carried a look that is usually reserved for people with real wealth, even though she didn't have that much money and came from a working-class background. She spotted Brent sitting at the window and made her way towards him. As she approached, Brent knocked his facial expression into neutral. He knew from experience that attempting to communicate with Eileen by smiling or frowning, or by using any other type of look, was risky. There was no telling how she would react. She would either ignore him or fire in a penetrating question. She might ask, "What are you smiling at?" It wouldn't be a pleasant enquiry. It would be more of a Gestapo-like interrogatory query. When she did this, it always caught Brent off-guard, which left him stammering and stumbling for an answer. Eileen maintained that communicating with your face should be left to the primates, not humans. "Why would you use your face to let anyone know what you're thinking or feeling? Surely this weakens your position and gives the other an advantage. It's a fool's practice," she'd say. Eileen only used facial expressions to communicate when she was being manipulative. Otherwise, she looked poker player deadpan. Her stare could unnerve the dead.

As Eileen came within a few feet, Brent thought that she knew; that she could see his forced appearance. He had to tuff it out. There was no going back now. He could feel his face muscles flicker and twitch in their efforts to betray his true feelings. He thought that it was a bit like trying not laugh, only in reverse. The thought of this took him to the verge of giggling. In turn, this conjured up an image of himself, gasping for breath with a bursting purple face. What a dilemma! He could either try to stay calm, fall to pieces and beg Eileen to let him off the hook or burst into hysterics. All these thoughts and feelings were too much, so his autonomous security mechanism whirred into life and the first whispers of a geeky theme tune and cheesy dialogue started to pipe up from catacombs that were his "safe place".

Eileen snapped him out of his trance and asked a question anyway. "Are you humming again Brent?"

"I wasn't aware of it Eileen……..How are you?............. You look great."

"I'm alright. I suppose…... Cheryl and that dog of hers have been around today. I wish she would get rid of that thing. It stinks."

"Yeah………. I know………… You look great"

"You're repeating yourself, Brent. Again. Tshhh."

"I wasn't aware of it Eileen……… This in nice though, eh?........... A Wednesday?"

Eileen knew that Brent was fishing to find out what she had in mind. So just for kicks, she toyed with him for the over the next half hour and two drinks. When she'd had her fun, she leaned over and beckoned him forward. He didn't need encouraged. She whispered her plans in his ear, and this time he was sure of it. Drips of urine definitely squirted from the end of his penis. On this occasion, it wasn't with fear.

He was right. Tonight was the night.

Brutus, Cheryl and Oslo

What's that smell?

Here we go again! Cheryl and Oslo are twittering on at each other with all the usual toing and froing and oo-ing and ahh-ing. They're trying on every outfit in their respective wardrobes while having a go at making each other's minds up about what to wear to the funeral. Oslo's prancing and twirling about the room, as per usual, trying his best to be as gay as humanly possible. I'll never understand that act. Why can't he just be as gay as he is? I don't think he knows that all humans are different. Even the gays ones. Some are gay-er than others. And some are less gay than others. It's the same for heterosexuals. So why can't Oslo just be as gay as he is? He's already topping the scale at the end of the gayness spectrum anyhow. Why does he need to try to break the barometer? Maybe someone should invent a gayrometer, a meter that measures the extent of a gay person's gayness. Gay people could have their gayness measured, and then act accordingly. It might prevent some of them from ridiculing and shaming themselves so much, then guzzling too many drugs and fucking too many people in an attempt to cover up it all up. What's the deal with the "I'm gay" statement anyway? "I'm gay and proud?" I understand the historical stigma and prejudice argument, and all that. But it's a bit old-fashioned, unless you live in Africa or Russia. No one really gives a shit in western culture nowadays, apart from the odd old homophobe or two who are still kicking about. So why be gay and proud? I'm a Chihuahua, and as I said earlier, I would pump anything. Even stuffed toys. And I'm bi-sexual. What would the other dogs think if I wore a t-shirt that said "Proud to be a bi-sexual Chihuahua?" "So what, mate," they'd bark.

"You're just a dog like the rest of us, and we've all got stuff going on in this life. Get over yourself, you self-indulgent crackerjack. You're not that important. Now give us a sniff of your arse and fuck off back to your handbag."

Oslo's telling Cheryl that the dress she's trying on isn't black enough. "It's not black-black, girlfriend" he poofily proclaims, while shaking his head from side to side and wagging his finger in the style of an obnoxious know-it-all, fat American black woman. "What would Grandpa Jack think about that dress, if he was alive today?" he bleated."

Grandpa Jack died of pancreatic cancer. He was Eileen's ex-husband's father. Eileen's ex-husband is Natalie's and Kevin's father, but not Cheryl's. Although Cheryl doesn't know that. Cheryl popped into the world nine months after one of Eileen's sex-quest sabbaticals back in the 80's, when she had youth on her side and her mother's stunning good looks. There's no denying that she's a first-class bitch, but she was supermodel material back in the day. Cheryl reckons that she can sing and act a bit too, but that's just a rumour. To prepare for her sex-quests in the past, she would start a fight with her ex-husband and turn his head inside out. Before you could say "shag me quick", she had fucked off somewhere exotic for a fortnight, while managing to make everyone else feel responsible for her pain. She would forgive them when she got back, and normal service resumed. Her ex-husband ran the numbers when Cheryl was born. He knew that she wasn't his. Eileen hadn't allowed him to have sex with her for at least a month after she returned from her so-called, mental breakdown. But, he was too shitty to say anything or do anything about it. Eileen had him in her grip. And they both knew it.

Cheryl and Oslo's fashion and accessory dilemma and the plastic drama that goes along with it, is a mind-numbingly repetitive scene that they play out every time they prepare to go out. The fact that someone is dead and that they're supposed to be attending a funeral to pay their respects means nothing to them. If they had the courage to tell the truth for once, they'd say "Fuck Grandpa Jack. Never liked the old bastard anyway. As long as we look good and get the chance to strut our stuff, then it'll be a good day for us." But they won't. They'll behave just like the rest of the faux-mourners. They'll nod and push their bottom lips out, and tilt their heads to the side a little, and say shit like, "ahhhh" or, "he had a good innings," or "at least he didn't suffer too much", or "it was nice service", or "wasn't the minister's speech nice!" No one will stand up and tell the truth. Especially the minister or priest, or whatever he is. They'd claim that it would be disrespectful. How do humans come up with such ridiculously stupid ideas? How can it be disrespectful to tell the truth? Everyone told the truth about Grandpa Jack behind his back when he was alive. Now he's dead, and its just not polite say it as it is? If I wasn't a dog, I'd go off to a monastery, or wherever these people go, and train to be a minister just for this one funeral. Can you imagine it? Father Brutus with the humongous nads. I'd walk out and take my place on the pulpit. Then I'd place both hands on either side of the big fat bible sitting on the podium in front of me. With my hands planted firmly in front of me, I'd bend my arms at the elbows lean in face first towards the fakes and phoneys. Then, I'd put on my best fire and brimstone expression and give them all an intense staring at for a good five minutes before saying a word. Just as they began to look around at each other in the hope that someone else might know what was going on, I'd let the have it. As loud as I could, I'd shout, "YOU"! while pointing my finger at no one in particular. Shit themselves, they would. When they were bolt-upright and paying heed, I'd then say, "now that I've got your attention, I'm gonna tell you the truth about Grandpa Jack. None of that laudatory bollocks during this epilogue my dear parishioners. We're gonna hear the wholesome. The whole truth and nothing but the truth. So help me, God. "Now, lets' have it right. You all know that Grandpa Jack was a hardworking, hard drinking, woodbine-stained, chain-smoking Glaswegian. And, that he was a dead ringer for Desperate Dan. Minus the red shirt, black waistcoat, cowboy hat and side shooter of course. And just like Dan, he had a big square jaw and stood bolt-upright. And just like Dan, he went about his daily business with an absolute not taking any shit from anyone attitude. And just like Dan, he backed this attitude up with the willingness, or stupidity, to fight anyone at the drop of a hat. Yet unlike Dan, he didn't eat cow pies. By all accounts, he was also a tyrannical child-beater who battered and psychologically and emotionally abused his kids and his wife. Other legends speak of him as a devout atheist, who ironically hated Catholics. On special occasions, he would attempt to disprove the existence of God by standing on the dining room table, and holding a fork aloft he would scream "STRIKE ME DOWN IF YOU'RE THERE YA CUNT!" When forked lightning failed to appear and electrocute him, he would turn to his audience, also known as his family, and sound his battle cry "SEE – FUCKING TOLD YEEZ." Parlour games in the sixties eh! Thank the lord they invented cheap alcohol, EastEnders and Facebook. However my dear brethren, outside the home, which meant at work or in the boozer, everyone thought he was a great guy. All forthright and proud he was. A stalwart.

Decked out in his immaculate suit, tie, tweed overcoat and infamous tartan cap, he would amaze and delight his audience by performing self-made magic tricks. He was the pub's darts champion and addressed every female as "sweetheart." By all accounts, a gentleman. Any trouble or arguments? He would knock his assailants clean out with his boxer's right hand while drinking shots of strong whiskey with his left. Classical Glaswegian box-office entertainment. The crowds loved him. Apart from that, he did nothing significant with his life. He pissed most of it up the wall and he wasn't shy about letting all of you know that he had no time for any of you. But unbeknownst to you all, he kept a secret from you. And he kept it because he knew you only too well. And he knew that he couldn't trust you with it. For all his hard-working and drinking, and alleged familial abuse and neglect, and fighting, and magic trickery, and atheistic tendencies, and for impersonating desperate Dan, he had a huge capacity for Love. And he gave it all to one of his grandsons. Your opinions on this matter are of no consequence. It doesn't matter if you believe it or not because this man's ability to Love saved his grandson's life. When his grandson was a child, he did something that no one knew about, until now. He walked with him. Every time he met this child, he performed the most emotionally elaborate and colourful celebration to let the child know he was glad to see him. Grandpa Jack jumped for joy like a little kid at Christmas, every time he saw this child. His delight was profoundly authentic. He wagged like a dog welcoming its master's return from a long journey, even if that child had only been out of the room for a few short minutes. He loved that child. And He loved him unconditionally. And he let that child, and everyone else around him know about it. But you people wouldn't have noticed. No one did. His actions told that child that he was totally entitled to be himself. His actions told that child that he was spectacularly amazing. His actions told that child that he was immensely worthy. His actions told that child that he shone like the brightest star. His actions liberated that child, if only for the briefest moments in his young tormented life. But most of all, amidst all the wreckage and carnage around him, and in spite of the hidden neglect and trauma and abuse that the child was being subjected to at the time, he managed to embed something in him. He reached into that child when no one else wanted to, and in doing so, he left behind an inextinguishable spark of love and hope. That spark was a force that the child lost touch with as he became an adult, but it would rise up again in later in life and come to his rescue when he needed it most. So, you see folks, Grandpa Jack might well have been a boozer, a grafter, an abusive man, a magician, a dandy character and an entertainer. But unbeknown to you lot, he was also one child's saviour. What's more, my dear brethren, he was an honest man and he never pretended to be anything or anyone else, other than who or what he was at any particular time". For my big finale, I'd re-adopt my fire and brimstone demeanour. And then, summoning all the skills and abilities that I'd learned in my training at the monastery, I'd leave them all feeling a little more guilty than they did before they came in by saying "now, can any of you lot say the same?" Quick as a wink, I'd finish and wave at the crowd before shooting through to the back of the alter and go rooting around the sacristy for any unsuspecting and particularly vulnerable altar boys to play with.

Grandpa Jack's funeral came and went without any excitement at all. Thirty or forty people turned up and as predicted, they said their piece and tipped their hats without really feeling much at all. When the average person dies, the people closest to them feel it the most. That's normally the immediate family members, like the wife, or husband, children and grandchildren and maybe even a few good friends. Probably between five and fifteen people will mourn and grieve with some seriousness. The rest of the funeral attendees, say another hundred if you're lucky, might feel saddened. Outside of that circle, the other seven billion people in the world will not give a shit one way or another. You humans are a strange breed that way. When you're alive, you tend to think about yourself all day long and the majority of you kill yourself with stress and anxiety in an attempt to achieve some sort of significance while you're breathing. But when the time comes and you pop your clogs, you'll be lucky if more than ten people shed a tear. A couple of heartbeats later and you'll be forgotten about, because nine of the ten tear shedders will be back in panic-land trying to grind out some sort meaning to their existence before they die next. And all the while, they'll do everything they can to hide from the fact that their time is coming. No one mourned properly for Grandpa Jack on that day, and that would have suited him just fine. His Grandson would've felt the loss. But he didn't know that his beloved Grandpa Jack had died because he was lost and no one had seen him for years. Thank fuck I'm not human after all. All I need to do is be overly interested in all other dogs and lick my own balls at every opportunity.

Cheryl and Oslo made it to the funeral. As usual, they were fashionably late. They made sure that the whole congregation saw them as they strode purposefully down the aisle to sit at the front of the church in the middle the clergyman's banal platitudes. A good strategy, they thought. Eventually, they had chosen to wear matching black-black outfits. Chez enlivened her garb by using me as a cosmetic addition to her look. The cow made me wear a fucking fake diamond encrusted collar and a matching black-black waistcoat to go with her Dolce and Gabana number. She gave up trying to get me to wear sunglasses when she woke up to the seriousness of my objections. She knows when I've had enough of that baloney, and she backs off accordingly. Not to let the side down, Oslo sported his best Hugo Boss black suit, and the tit wore alligator-skinned cowboy boots tucked under his trousers with a sparkly buckle mounted on the side of them. He said that the buckle's glint would catch the light and complement my necklace and Chez's earrings at the same time. They both agreed that only the real fashion conscious would notice the subtly of their sophisticated, stylistic touch. To applaud themselves and cement their smug sense of self-satisfaction, they gave each other a single nod of the head and accompanied it with verbal hmmfff, all in perfect synchronicity. Just when I thought I'd seen it all, this pair of dingbats did something that proves how self-indulgence and self-entitlement have taken root in the psyche of the masses and become the norm. When the sermon ended and everyone was filing out of the church in an orderly fashion, Chez an Oslo held back and took a joint selfie with the coffin showing behind them. They didn't put on the immortalised "selfie pout", which we all know was invented by Ben Stiller in the film Zoolander when he did "blue steel." Instead, they contorted their coupons in an attempt to look forlorn and saddened. It didn't go as planned. The macabre pose gave them the appearance of a couple of deranged body snatchers who were happy to have found their latest trophy. The dynamic duo managed to get my mush into the pic to, by squishing my head between theirs for the shot. If you looked closely enough, you can tell that I'm not the happiest pup on the planet. If given the chance, I'd strangle both of them with the blingy collar they made me wear. The eerie selfie received nine hundred and twenty-two likes on Facebook and Chez and Oslo delighted in another successful venture.

Natalie and Chad

"Natalie?"

"What Chad?"

"Have you heard about the term Millennials?"

"Yes, hun. I've been keeping an eye on that. Why do you ask ?"

"I was talking to Joe the other day, and he asked me if knew anything about it. He's been hearing different stories about the subject. Some good, some bad. He's a bit mixed up, because he's not sure what it really means to be one. He said, "Dad, am I a millennial? Does this mean that I'm nasty and lazy, or not?" I told him I'd talk to you about it and get back to him. What do you think babe? What's your take on it?

"I think it's really interesting. Have you see new mobile phone advert on the telly, where the twenty-something girl talks about being a Millennial and how good it all is? She's dressed like a rainbow with green and blue hair, and she's all smiley miley. She's really irritating."

"I haven't seen it, or her. Do you think it's a good thing or bad thing?"

"Both"

"I love our conversations, you know. But you………are a purple plum. One that sits high up in its tree. C'mon then Ms Ghandi. Tell us what you mean."

"It's a good bad, bad thing. Init?"

"Be serious Natalie. This is the now-generation and the future one. Our kids are heading straight into it. I don't have a clue about this stuff. You're the floaty thinker in the family. What's your take on it?"

"Ok, You win. Here we go. I was watching a youtube video about it, by kind of American psychologist, or something. I'm not sure. Anyway, the guy seemed to be well up on the subject. He talks about the pros and cons of being a Millennial and how employers need to gear-up for them because of the way they are. He also talks about their characters. How they are very impatient, shit at relationships and they believe that they deserve to have whatever they like, without putting in any effort to get it. I especially like the section where he talks about how they got that way in the first place. He blames most of it on parenting. Basically, he says that parents have spoiled them. I'm not so sure about that theory, or the one where he reckons that employers need to learn to understand them though. I think he's missing the mark."

"Why like? What do you think employers should do?"

"I don't know. But I don't think pandering to their dysfunctional characteristics is going to help the situation."

"What do you think will help?"

"Looking at and understanding the whole story. Not just blaming the last round of parents in the evolutionary chain. The youtube guy doesn't even mention grandparents. Not that it's totally the parent's fault anyway. He only talks about the reality of being a Millennial and offers a few suggestion on how to work with them, without fully exploring and trying to totally understand the wider issues in the first place. He's only offering up half the job. That's my opinion anyway."

"You think?"

"Yeah. I do"

"I know I don't need to ask, but I will anyway."

"Eh….thanks…..I think"

"Shut up daft arse. Listen. What 's your opinion on the whole story then? If I think that I know what you're saying, and I think I do, then you think there' s more to it than just parenting."

"That's a lot of thinking and knowing in the one sentence Chad. Did you stop for breath there?"

"Arsehole. Answer the question. You know what I mean."

"Right. I think it has more to do with violence and economics, than parenting. I think those two are the real culprits. After all the question is, why are most Millennials the way they are.? Why are they self-entitled, lazy buggers with no work ethic, who can't handle real relationships? Sticking the blame for all of that on parenting isn't fair. Don't you need to ask why the parents spoiled them in the first place? I think you do."

"Ok. I'll be devil's advocate. Why did the parents spoil them in the first place?"

"I told you. Violence and economics. Simple."

"You're a tool, Nat."

"I know. It's my favourite thing about me.

"Tell me about the violence part of your theory then."

"Well, I was wondering why I believe that it's not OK to hit our kids, yet I think it's acceptable that my mother hit me, even if it was just a tap on the back of the hand or a smacked backside. I know that she was emotionally abusive but when it comes to physical punishment, I felt as if I was contradicting myself. On one hand, I was saying that hitting kids is understandable and on the other, I was saying it's absolutely not. Then all of a sudden, it dawned on me. If I wanted my head to stop spinning and to stop feeling so weird about it, then I needed to make a decision one way or another. Obviously, there were only two choices. Either it's OK to hit kids or it's not. As you can imagine, it was an easy decision. I decided that it's definitely not. As soon as I made that decision, I became really, really angry. I started thinking about Eileen and how she had no right to do what she did, no matter what her intentions were. I thought that her nastiness hadn't touched me. I thought that I had escaped her. It took everything I had not to call her right there and then and give her mouthful down the phone."

"You've never told me about this."

"I know. I haven't avoided the conversation. It just hasn't come up, until now."

"I get what you mean now Nat, about punishing children. But I still don't know what that's got to do with Millennials and their self-entitlement, laziness and neediness."

"What I'm saying is, that our parents lived in an age where physically punishing children was normal. They were even allowed to use belts, slippers and canes. It was legal. And that's only one generation away. The further you go back in time, the worse it gets. You know what older people are like. They go on about how hard it was for them, and how kids have it easy nowadays. You and I say the same thing. We couldn't have dreamed up some of the things that kids get up to today in comparison to us when we were children, never mind the generations before us. Mobile phones are the prime example. Kids believe that they have the right to mobile phone and a contract without working for it. So do the parents. Look at our Joe. Even Tilly's got her eye on a new i-phone. She's only 11 ! And we'll need to get her one or face the consequences."

"I still don't get it, Nat. What am I missing?"

"I'm saying that parents spoil their kids today because of their past. It's hereditary. They believe that their kids deserve to get the things they never had. Then, they think their children won't suffer as much as they did. After all, who wants to see their children suffering? But, I don't think that's the case. I think parents spoil their kids to stop themselves from seeing and feeling the reality of the violent world that they grew up in. It was only less than thirty years ago when all children knew that adults were allowed to assault them with weapons. Can you imagine what that must have been like as small child? Even today, the law in England says you have the right to hit your child, and children know it."

"Let's see if I understand this. You're saying that Millennials have been spoiled because their parents don't want to see and feel the truth about their own past."

"Exactly. That's the violence part. Even you and I were hit as children, yet we defended our parents by saying that it wasn't that bad. But now, we know different. It's unbearable for most adults to even contemplate that there might be some truth to this. If you get into a discussion with them about it, they act as if they know it all already, or they just poo-poo the idea and walk away. I'm' telling you. Try it. Look, I'll give you an example of how this works."

"Go on then."

"Right then. I will. Who came up with the idea that participating in a school sports is just as good as winning it, therefore everyone should get a medal?"

"I don't know Nat, but I'm sure you're about to tell me."

"Of course I am. It was a group of adults who were shit at school sports. They couldn't bear to look at the poor faces of the little losers because it reminded them of themselves. So, they changed the game to fix their pain. What a de-motivator that is. Getting a medal, whether you try hard or not."

"There's no violence in that example, Nat."

"I know. But it works on the same principle. And it's much easier to get an adult to admit that they were shit at school sports before they'll admit that their parents were abusive. If they agree that hitting kids is abusive now, and they were hit when they were kids, then they need to see themselves as abused and see their parents as abusers. It's a chunky pill to chew and swallow."

"Your idea sounds plausible."

"Why thank you darling. You know how I while away on these subjects for hours."

"What about the economics thing then? You said Millennials are the way they are because of violence and economics."

"I did indeed, I did."

"C'mon then. Share with the group."

"You know about the Great Depression back in the twenties and thirties in America, don't you?"

"I've seen the old black and white films and some of the documentaries about it. So, yes. I do."

"The financial markets and banks crashed, most people lost their jobs and the country was on its knees for about ten years. But the people at the top, with the real money, were never affected that much. In fact, they made a profit from it. Zoom forward to 2008, when the exact same thing happened and governments across the world bailed the banks out this time. Right?"

"Right"

"Right. It's simple. The economy wasn't allowed to collapse this time because it was more profitable to keep it running. It was just a numbers game. And how was it more profitable to keep it running, I hear you ask? Well, I'll tell you. Because of the amount of money that parents spend on their kids. Obviously, that's only a small part of the story. Proper economists will say I'm talking baloney, but it's an important part of understanding why Millenials are the way they are. It ties into the violence argument. By that I mean, that most modern parents think buying their kids the best of stuff will stop them from suffering. Again, they can't bear to see them suffering because it reminds them of their own suffering when they were children. On top of all of that, both parents and their children are under tremendous pressure to buy stuff because clever marketers tell them that they will suffer even more if they don't. Does this make sense Chad, or am I rambling again?"

"No Nat. You're not rambling. It's a good argument and it makes sense. I need to pick the kids up from school. I'll see you when I get back"

"Ok then. Don't buy them anything and don't hit them!"

"I do love you. But you are a fanny."

Kevin

It's Monday morning. Concerns Group time.

"Sonny Boy?"

"Sonny Boy?"

"Can we get to fuck out of here?... Please!"

"These cunts are cunts... It's no use anyway... it's time to hit the streeeet... we can bolt back to Jo'burg... be there in no time... the Numbers gang will have forgotten all about you by now... please, Sonny Boy ... let's go... you fanny bag... it's only a matter of time ... me- 'n - u ... back on the gear... the inevitable is inevitable, Sonny Boy ... always has been ... always will be..."

The Concerns Group is when all the residents in the rehab get together in one big room, with staff in attendance. The idea is that we raise concerns about each other's safety and welfare. The way it works is, each person gets a chance to say who he or she is concerned about, and why. In reality, it's just a big fuck-fest. Not the kind where we all take our clothes off, cover ourselves with chocolate flavoured olive oil and bonk each other to death. It's the psychological and emotional warfare kind. You've got a mix of thirty drug addicts and alcoholics sitting in the same room, and each and every one of them is shitting a brick about who's going to get the spotlight jammed up their nose first. Two weeks ago, most of these degenerates were running around city centres, robbing-and-a-stabbing and shooting-and-a-tooting for a skag-bag. Or a bottle of White Lightning. All of a sudden, they've become experts on each other's triggers to relapse and sub-conscious behavioural traits and avoidance strategies. As fucking if? I don't know what's worse. The idea that any one of these dingoes might get to find out about some of my vulnerabilities, or the fact that the staff are supposed to be looking after me. If the staff were looking after me, they wouldn't let half of one of these nutcases anywhere near me. I'm saying fuck all. To everybody.

"That's the spirit Sonny Boy... sounds a bit more like it... like it..."

We're all sitting on hard-backed chairs in a big circle, waiting on three staff members to arrive. They do this every Monday. Keep us waiting until they arrive through the door, all at the same time and all dressed in black. They dress in black every other day of the week too. Not just on Monday mornings. What the fuck? Rumour mongers say, that they dress that way to prevent us residents from developing unhealthy emotional attachments to them. That's all well and good, but at the same time it doesn't inspire a sense of faith and trust in these supposed helpers. It just makes them look and feel like powerful authority figures. You'd think that a team of therapists would understand why police and priests dress in black? Obviously not. Their appearance scares the living daylights out of me. What a strange saying? I don't know where I pick these things up, or why I use them. The Black Brigade have entered the room. It's tumbleweed time. The tension and anxiety reeks. Its visible as well. I can't keep my eyes off of three or four particularly scheming scum-fuckers who have been on my case from the moment I walked through the door. They mooch about in little clique. Residents that is, not staff. Even on my first few days, they were raising concerns about me in groups. They tried to disguise their intentions by saying they were worried about the safety of the community, as they thought I must have smuggled some drugs into the rehab when I was admitted, because I looked "overmedicated," as they put it. Who knows what they are up to? They're up to something though, and it's no good. The residents refer to themselves as a community, but there's not an ounce of communal, shared purpose to be found amongst them. Real community values are definitely not woven into the fabric that underpins this pack of wolves. Most of them only gave up the drugging and mugging grannies last Wednesday. Now, they're trying to convince themselves and everyone else that they're benevolent, philanthropic altruists. Paul Daniels couldn't pull off a trick like that, but somehow these fuckers are almost believable. It's a well-known fact, in junkie circles that is, that most drug addicts possess and waste an inordinate amount of talent in comparison to their counterparts. Normal, everyday, taxpaying consumers, that is. Sales skills and deception figure in their top three most squandered attributes. There's an old joke, that goes like this. What's the difference between a drug addict and an alcoholic? They'll both steal your money, but the drug addict will help you look for it and console you when you don't find it. This place is filled with a mixture of both. Both sexes too. It's a fucking riot. Really. It is. The junkies hate the alkies and the alkies hate the junkies. One side attend Alcoholics Anonymous groups and the other attend Narcotics Anonymous groups. Rival factions in a world of wasters, where each fight relentlessly for the moral high ground. The alkies are the best laugh. They stand atop their rivals and looking down, they label the junkies as disease-carrying, injecting, purse-snatching vermin. They console themselves in the fact that they only pissed and shit in their trousers once a fortnight and occasionally battered their wives and kids before blacking out. The junkies just don't like the alkies, because that's what the majority of their parents were. Most of the junkies tell you that they'll be able to have drink when they leave rehab, because they've never had a problem with it. It's only weak people that get addicted to alcohol, they cry. I suppose both groups are just like any other class of people. They always look down the social scale, never up it, to solidify their okay-ness. It's an international tune, and it goes like this. "Well, at least I'm not that bad!"

The three or foursome that I have been keeping an eye on are murmuring away to each other about something. Probably someone, not some-thing. The leader of the Musketeers is a Cockney dwarf. He's not real dwarf. But he's close. He's all "inint bruv" and rhyming slang. He sounds like a two-stroke motocross bike, and has the presence and energy of an injured wasp. He revels in indiscriminately spearing other people with his venomous sting. I ignore or avoid him whenever I can. Unfortunately, I'm a member of the group that lives here, which means I have to sit at their picnic table. So, his stings and smarting welts are inevitable. When he talks, he points everywhere at the same time with both hands. If you turned the volume down while he gibbers on, you'd think he was directing aircraft up the runway. During his rants, which never halt, his eyes rapidly dart to and from every corner of the room. I think he's expecting to get run over by a stray aeroplane. It's more likely to be a habitual hangover from his years of thieving and ripping off people who are inclined to throw you in the back of a van, take you down a country road, put your legs across a drainage ditch, and fold your knees back to front with a sledgehammer. He's always telling stories about his daring-do's, and for some reason I'm inclined to believe him. He might be unsavoury, but he doesn't strike me as a liar. I wasn't here at the time, but legend has it that he told everyone a tale about his antics when he was only six or seven years old. One day, for reasons known only to him and the world's best child psychologists, he decided to show everyone in the school playground what his shit looked like as it emerged into the world from his arsehole. Promptly, he dropped his shorts and skids, lay on his back, hooked his arms around and under his knees, lifted his bare bum in the air, pulled his cheeks apart and produced the turtles head for all to see. Then in a flash, he pulled of some sort of mystical yogic feat and whipped the pokey, protruding turd right back to where it came from. From the delight he expressed at his ingenuity, you'd be forgiven for thinking he'd won an Olympic gold medal. I stood there bewildered and amazed at the tale. It wasn't the kind of thing you could make up. His second in command is also a Londoner. I call him Greasy Weasel – Batman's Robin. His hair is almost blonde and amasses itself around his head in a big bunch of tightly bound curls. He suits his anaemic complexion, but his sharp pointy nose and beady eyes are far too close together. They give him a bit of predatory look. Not the predatory grace you might see when looking at a Golden Eagle. It was more akin to the exploitative hunger displayed by Oliver Twist's Fagan. He walks and talks in a similar fashion to Fagan too. All curling fingers and menacing intent, with creepy undertones. If you imagine Mr Burns from The Simpsons with blonde curly hair, then you'll get an idea of the picture I see. He's only nineteen and he comes from money. Which means he's one of the only two cash paying customers in the building, and he's not shy about letting people know it. The rest of us are here at the discretion of the state. He isn't as abrasive or as overtly bullying as his shit-showing leader, but he's skilled at making sure that the clique's malicious intent hits its target without anyone else taking too much notice of him. He's a particularly unusual character. Difficult to figure out. Gossipers say that he's never been involved in an intimate or sexual relationship of any kind. Strange bod. Needs watching.

"Sonny Boy…………………….they all need fucking watching…When are we off?"

The third crewmember is a girl. Well, a young woman. For some reason, she appears as a girl to me. Mid to late twenties. Dark, short hair. She fronts a hard, knotty facial expression that masks her stunning good looks. I listened to her life story when she read it out, so I know why her face looks the way it does. Throughout her childhood, she was systematically abused and raped by a male family member. Her mother knew about it but pretended she didn't. On telling her life story, she disclosed all of the physical, emotional and psychological suffering that she endured as a young child, aged only four or five. Her ordeal ended when she was eleven or twelve. From then on, her life was littered with tales of drug use, prostitution, crime and prison. I don't think I've ever heard anything as sad. Everyone reads his or her life story out in front of the whole community. It's mandatory.

"Not for us it's not Sonny Boy ……………..no ……...fucking ……..way – ski…"

Of all the stories that I've heard so far, hers was the most touching. It's no wonder she became a drug addict. Naysayers bleat about drug addiction being a cop-out, because other people have suffered similar fates yet they never turned out to be drug addicts. I say go fuck yourself, and try living in her shoes for a day. I think she's a captive in that group of bandits, mainly because of the Millwall Midget. He's a schmoozer and a fast talker. For a short-arse he surprisingly handsome, and there's no escaping his charismatic magnetism. Still, the same thing was said about Ted Bundy and his kind. I imagine he's praying on her vulnerability and keeping her onside as an emotional hostage. If he gets the chance, he'll fuck her and dump her as soon as he's had his fill. Greasy Weasel will be right behind him, cheering him on. The fourth member of the group is another male. Simon the Jam boy. Jam boys were young male slaves back in the eighteen hundreds, or thereabouts. Usually, they were aged between eight and ten. Whenever their rich plantation owners held a party or went on a pleasure excursion of some kind, like golfing, they would take the jam boys with them. They were called jam boys because their masters would cover them in jam, to keep the flies and insects away from them and their friends as they played. Jam boy is Tottenham's Tiniest's gofer. He runs around making tea, cadging smokes and gathering intel on the rest of the community for his boss. At first I thought he was another vulnerable, victim type. But after observing him for a few weeks, I came to the conclusion that enjoys his job. A little too much, if you ask me. He doesn't say much. When he moves about the building, he reminds me Dr Frankenstein's lab assistant, Egor. Minus the big hump, bulging beady eyes and crooked nose.

The staff team have just arrived on the scene, and they're semi-wise to this bunches' capers. So, they split them up right away and make them sit in seats far apart from each other. It's obvious that this distresses the girl more than the other three. She's on her own now. Her safety net has had a big hole cut in it. What are the people who run this place thinking about? She doesn't need to be here. Not yet, anyway. Not until she develops some resilience. It's a male-dominated, hostile and aggressive environment. If I could help her, I would. I want to go over and sit with her. She obviously needs some comfort and security. She needs help. The therapists might think that this environment will strengthen her in some way. I suppose it might. But who the fuck are they to risk it? What if it doesn't ? What if it tips her over the edge and she goes back to the street?

The staff team start the group in the usual way. The newcomers don't know what to expect. Those of us who have been here for a while, do. The senior staff member fires the starting pistol, and says "It's your community?" That's it. Right away, the Shoreditch Shorty shoots out of trap three, gunning for the rabbit. He picks on one of the newcomers. A scrawny little guy who has just fallen through the door after a fifteen year stint of injecting anything he can find into any available vein. No doubt, like me, he's a groin injector. By the way he looks, he'll be lucky to keep all of his limbs. He's mid-detox and rattling like a bean can full of pebbles. Cunty Cockney announces that he is concerned about the newbie, because he thinks that he has brought drugs into the community, because he looks over medicated. That old chestnut. Then he turns to the senior staff member and nods. The senior staff member nods back in acknowledgment. What the fuck? How did that alliance come about? The rattler lowers his head in shame at himself, and whispers something in his defence. Another staff member steps in and puts the question to him again, more directly this time. "Did YOU bring any drugs into the building on admission?" Give the guy his due, he stepped out of his slump for a second and fired back, "Fuck off. Do you think I would be in this fucking condition if I had any drugs? I thought you people were supposed to be experienced. Leave me alone, I'm fucking ill. Are you blind?" I nearly jumped out of my seat and started cheering for the underdog. The Muswell Munchkin had other ideas. I've watched him over the past eight weeks. If he keeps shooting a blanket of rapid-fire-concerns at the thirty other group members, then it wont be long before the two hour session is up, and he can escape untouched. It's a good strategy. All week long, his hump-less messenger has been feeding him with all the goodies and gossip on the rest of us. The staff treat him like a superstar, because a lot of the concerns he raises are valid. Not in the sense that they are helpful to anyone in any way. But, they are all close to the truth. A three-strike system shores-up the rules and regulations. A single strike gets dished out for any breach of contract. I was given one on my second week, for drinking caffeinated coffee in town. No caffeine allowed. If you are given a third strike, the staff march you up to your room, make you pack your clothes and belongings and escort you to the train station on the spot. No if's or but's. You're gone. The community know this, and they're no angels. They're junkies and alkies. They've been fucking about with rules from the moment they stepped on the premises. The top four don't do's are; no shagging, pornography, violence or threatening behaviour and no drugs or alcohol, obviously. These are the cardinal sins. Where did I get that one? A cardinal sin? Break any of these, and you're hoofed out the door there and then. This bunch of misfits have closets full of skeletons, and they know only too well that the Cockney and his cronies have the low-down and dirty on them all. This means that they're afraid to raise any valid concerns against that fearsome foursome, in case of get-backs. So here I am. In amongst this shit. Salvos are shooting across the room in all directions. Cockney and crew have instigated most of it. When they finished with the detoxer, they throw a grenade at one of the red-nosed gang. No, not the reindeers. The alkies. They said that one of them had bought a steak and ale pie for his lunch on a visit to town. And this, they claimed, could be the first step on the road to relapse. The fucking staff actually took it serious, purporting all kinds of SID's. SID's is one of the many acronyms that they use here. It means, a Seemingly Insignificant Decision. The alky wasn't your stereotypical cider hugging street dweller. He's been about a bit. Seen a bit. And done a bit. I heard his life story too. He was on probation for robbing a charity of nearly half a million quid. The grenade launchers accused him of being here on a jail swerve and that he wasn't a real alky. Who knows? Anyway, he's an angry dude. He comes right back, full blast at his accusers and the staff. "Are you morons having a fucking laugh?" he screams, while the rest of his face turned as red as his nose. "Steak and ale fucking pie? Fucking steak and fucking ale fucking pie? Really? I don't know whose worse? You four fuckers" pointing to his accusers "or you fucking ding dongs for listening to them," pointing to the staff. Aha. An ally. At last. Someone who's not got anything to hide from these conniving cunts, the residents that is, not the staff. And he doesn't seem as afraid I am. I'll grab him later for a chat. For the next two hours, the bombs were lobbed and landed, and lobbed and landed back again. I can't say if anything meaningful was achieved. It was just a relief to get it over and done with. See you all next week. Same place, same time.

As I'm walking out the door, the Cockney invites me to his room for some reason. Being in someone else's room is against the rules. Fuck it. I want to hear what he has to say.

I've got two strikes left and I'm prepared to risk one of them. As I go through the door, his pals follow behind me. I'm nervous.

"Right Sonny boy, first things first......................listen up and listen good..................if any of these pond-life dwellers try anything......................then don't run..............you know the dance........................no matter what ....don't fucking run..........their gaffer gets it first ....got it?"

"Got it."

"What did you say?" says cockers

"Nothing, I was talking to myself"

"Oh. Never mind." He says. He follow this up with, "You'll never guess what we did during the community group?" and he turns to look at his entourage for approval. And they give him it, by nodding and hmmmmmm-ing and yes-ing all over the shop, just like he trained them to. At the same time, they start tittering and giggling like schoolkids.

"You're right, I'll never guess," I say, as my mouth goes bone dry.

"Sonny Boy..............................head-butt this cunt right on the bridge of the nose if he so much as farts upwind............................got it?"

"Got it."

"What did you say?", says cockers

I come back with "What, sorry, what?" pretending that I don't know what he's talking about, and I feel my left foot making its way behind my right. When I was young I did a bit of boxing, so I know I'm making an offensive stance and preparing to crack cockney's snib if he makes a wrong move. I don't like this about myself. I'm shitting it now.

"Will I tell him?" he says, looking to his minions again for approval. They nod in unison, and gleefully bang the heels of their hands together like hungry seals. "You'll never guess what?" he says again. This time I don't respond. I just wait, as I know he's going to tell me anyway.

"Get ready ………sonny boy………..NO prisoners   !"

He starts by saying, "We snuck into Siobhan's room five minutes before the community group, when everyone was gathering in the lounge…….." Siobhan is a twenty-one year old Irish girl, who just came in last week. She was the other cash-paying customer in the rehab. The drugs hadn't taken their toll on her yet, like most other females here, so, she still has her looks, her teeth and her figure. She has expensive clothes as well. "……and Alan…." AKA Greasy Weasel…" robbed a pair of her lacy knickers from her top drawer. And you'll never guess what? He wore them throughout the whole community group. Just for a dare." They all burst into fits of laughter. I'm lost. Why the fuck are they telling me this? Do they think that I think this is funny? Are they trying to recruit me into their gang? What the fuck is going on here? Then I start laughing along with them. I can hear and see myself laughing. And I cringe. But I keep laughing anyway. I figure it out. It's funny and not funny at the same time. But I don't know which one to choose. I make the excuse that I need to go, in case I get a strike for being in the room. They give me some good-old-boy pats and slaps on the back as I leave. I don't whether to vomit or go back and set about the three of them. Not the girl. I just feel terrible for her. The other three, though.

"Do it Sonny boy………………………………….don't be fud…………………get back in there and get these cunts told…………………….sharpish…………………..you know you've been stitched up…………………they've got you now…………………you know something about them…………………and if you don't grass them up to the staff………………then you're guilty by association…………………do something ………………..you banana cake…………………fucking do something…………….kick them to fuck……………..or stick them in it…………………but do fucking something ………………you shit bag!…………………get us fucking out of here……………….C'mon Sonny boy ……………………….let's fucking go!"

Fuck this. I'm off. I'm not sticking about here for another minute. Fuck this. I'm off. I'm off……………….I'm off…………..

Why am I looking up the stairs when I cant remember coming down them. Why am I lying on the deck? Why does my back and neck hurt so much? Why is Mike leaning over me and asking if I'm OK ?

Why is the light fading?   Am I asleep?

Kevin and Mike

"Hi Kevin"

"Hi, Mike."

"Thanks for attending our session today. It's good to see you."

Thanks, Mike. It's good to see you too."

"How's your life story coming along? Have you written much yet?"

"No. Nothing"

"Are you finding it difficult?"

"No. I'm not doing it."

"Why not?"

"That's my decision. I'm not prepared to explain it any further. Sorry, Mike. I don't mean to be an arsehole."

"It's unusual Kevin. Most people have a go at it. You know it's a compulsory part of your programme while you're staying here?"

"Yes, Mike. I know. I'm prepared to accept the consequences."

"Even if it means going to prison? You know what the magistrate said."

"I know. I'm not putting those words on paper. I can't. I won't."

"I like you, Kevin. I've worked with tens of hundreds of drug addicts and alcoholics over the years and I've seen stubbornness and wilfulness in all of them. I don't think you're like that though. I'd really like to understand why you won't write your story. Can you read and write OK?"

"Yes. I don't have a problem with that. I don't know how to explain it. I just know that it's not going to happen. I understand your position, Mike. Really, I do."

"Ok, Kevin. Do you think you could verbalise it?"

"Yes. No problem. I suppose that's the thing. It only needs to be said once. After that, it'll be done. Gone. It'll never need saying again. Writing it down would mean reading it again. It will lose its vitality and authenticity. Surely the spoken word has no equal in that way?"

"Maybe Kevin? I don't know. Do you want to start it now?"

"Yes."

"OK then. Let's start with your earliest memories."

"It's funny. My first memories are mostly sensations. Not people or places or things. They come afterwards. The first thing I remember, is the feeling of the cloth material that covered the sofa I lay on as a child. I don't have any idea what age I was at the time. I could have been two, three, four or five years old. I don't know. I remember a small, black and white panda bear. A soft toy. I remember the feeling of its fur and the hardness of its glass eyes. I liked its eyes. They fascinated me. I remember happiness, because I was wearing a cowboy suit, and standing at the top of a hill on a street in a council housing estate. I remember feeling afraid in bed. Staring at the bedroom door, wondering if a bogeyman was hiding behind it. I remember a head, with a hat, popping around the door and it looked at me. I dived under the covers. I don't know if it was real or a dream. I remember dreaming about hundreds of fish eating my toes. I woke up screaming about the fishes and how they were coming to get me. I remember kindness. Was it my mother comforting me about the dream? I don't know if it was her. I still don't like my feet hanging out the end of the bed today. I need them covered. I remember hearing the screaming and shouting. My mother and father going at each other about money. I remember panicking, "What about me? Don't forget about me!" I remember my father's drinking and hangovers. How he lay in bed, still half drunk, and how he sent me to my mother with sarcastic messages for her. I was innocent. I thought it was a game. I thought he was being playful. I remember my mother's face. Her anger at me. He's set me up so that she would leave him alone. He knew her, and he knew how she would respond. I remember my sister. We were babies. Less than three years of four years old. We were inseparable. I remember playing in the street. I remember running. I was faster than everyone else. I remember my first day at school. Other kids were crying for their mothers as they left them. I remember wondering what was wrong with them. I remember thinking that they should know how to look after themselves. Why cry for your mother? It didn't make sense. I remember wondering. I've always wondered. I still wonder. That was my first memory of it. I remember wondering what would happen if I ran my finger down a crack in a glass window. I remember the shock and surprise as I sliced my own finger open. I remember wondering what would happen if I sucked water from a muddy puddle through a length of rubber pipe. I remember the shock and surprise at my mouth filling with muddy puddle water and dirt. I remember wondering what would happen if I shoved a one-inch piece of crayon up my nose. I remember screaming as it disappeared out of reach, and the kindness of the teacher who helped me blow out back out into a handkerchief. I remember watching my mother hang over the sink, vomiting for hours because she had an ulcer. I remember panicking, "What about me? Don't forget about me!" I remember my father quizzing me about my mother and her whereabouts. I felt like a traitor, but at the same time duty-bound to answer him. I remember him hitting me and my sister for fighting. We must've been four or five years old. I remember our screams. I remember Catholic Churches and being forced to say prayers every day. I didn't want to say prayers. I didn't like them. I thought the priest was telling lies. I didn't believe anything he said. I remember my father screaming about blasphemy. I remember my father's art. He was a fabulous artist. He would draw for me sometimes, if I asked him. I remember all the kids in the street where I grew up. There must have been twenty of us. They were all Protestants. I was the only Catholic. I remember wondering, "What is wrong with me?" A question I asked myself, a lot. I remember asking the schoolteacher if she thought I was fat. "No", she said. "You're just cuddly." I remember thinking she was a liar. I remember telling my family members about it, and I remember the sound of their laughter. I remember sadness, bewilderment, loneliness, despair and feeling utterly lost. I remember fighting with other kids and feeling OK about it. I remember my mother calling me bad, and threatening me for fighting. I remember how she corralled me into a corner, and she didn't let up until I promised never to fight again. I remember collecting trinkets and odds and ends around the house and finding a little tin box to put them in. I remember my mother snatching the box away from me, and saying, "What the fuck do you think you're doing, sonny boy?" I remember imploding. I felt as if a bomb had just went of inside me. I remember spiralling inwards while my head fell forwards, till my chin touched my chest. I remember visiting the dentist. I remember he looked like an evil doctor from an old horror film. I must've been six, seven or eight years old. I can't remember. I remember my mother had left me there on my own, because she had shopping to do. I remember the dentist putting me in the chair, as I started to cry with fear. I remember him grabbing me by the hood of my jacket and the choking as he lifted me out of the chair. I remember him tossing me out into the street without saying a word. I remember waiting for my mother's return. I remember her asking me what had happened and her tuts of disgust as she walked away when I told her. She knew I had to follow her. I remember my siblings. I remember feeling nothing for them. I remember feeling nothing. I remember numbness. A lot. I remember dancing and how it happened all on its own. For me, on rare occasions, I danced with no forethought. When I stopped, people clapped. I remember feeling ashamed. I remember my extended family. All the aunts, uncles and cousins. I remember walking alone, often. I remember the canals, the bridges, the weeds, algae and the green grassy embankments. I remember swimming there with my friends, and the fear of fish biting my toes. I didn't swim there again. I remember the school bully. This wasn't your everyday, bog-standard school bully. This guy was a fucking animal. And he looked, moved, walked and talked like one. At around ten years old, he had the body of a teenage bear. This guy slashed other kids with pencil sharpener blades. He tied them up with rope and threw them off garage roofs. He bludgeoned them with the thick, metal pellet-gun handles. And he laughed with a vicious giggle. He got me in his sights and caught me in his grip a few times. I remember fantasising about blowing him up with a hand grenade. Not that I would ever have done it. I had made a promise never to fight again, and I didn't have a grenade. I lived in abject terror at the thought of him, until my early teens. I remember staring out at the world through the big window in junior school. I remember my article on butterflies, and when it was published in the school magazine. I remember feeling pride. I remember hating football. All the other boys loved it. I remember being picked last in the lineout for football games. I remember moments of greatness on the football field, and how the good players were amazed by my performance. I was amazed too. I remember the red ash football fields, and the grazes and burns on my arms and legs. I remember my indifference to physical bumps and sprains. I remember slashing myself across the back of the hand with a piece of glass, because I didn't want to face the bully at school. I remember the shock, as the wound opened up in front of my eyes, and the thoughts that I had went too far. I remember my mother bandaging it, as I told her it was an accident. I remember having my hair washed and my back scratched. I remember touch, and how I yearned for it, but rarely got it. I remember fighting again, because a boy challenged me in front of everyone. I remember rage. I remember stamping on his head and trying to kill him. I remember righteousness. I remember the school bully intervening and stopping me, by smashing me over the head with a pair of football boots, studs first. I remember wondering, "Why did he do that?" I thought he would have found my fierceness admirable. I remember my disdain and utter lack of compassion, as I walked away from the boy I had left bleeding on the grass. I remember crying for myself, because of what I had become and what I had done. I remember emptiness. I remember my first conscious taste of alcohol. I remember knowing that this was for me. I had found a friend. I remember the wait, until next time. I remember anticipation. I remember my first kiss. I remember feeling locked in. I remember wanting someone to take care of me. I believe that if they knew what is what like to be me, then they would want to take care of me. I remember profound self-pity. I remember stealing apples. I remember stealing. I liked it. I remember knocking on the front door to my house. I remember my little aunt, standing there with tears streaming down her face. I remember her words "Your daddy's gone." I remember loss, and how it pulled down and away in the pit of my stomach. I remember the crying and wailing as I walked into the sitting room. I remember my sister at my mother's feet. I remember panicking, "What about me? Don't forget about me!" I remember the adults telling me that I was the man of the house now. I remember feeling like a child. I remember crying on my own, but not for the loss of a father. He was never that. I cried for me. I remember walking alone, alongside the canals, bridges, reeds, weeds and pathways. I remember playing truant. I remember defiance. I remember the schoolteachers in the first years of high school. I remember indifference and violence. I remember staring out through the big glass school windows that were full of holes, because golf balls came through them at lunch break. Not that it was close to a golf course. The school kids did it. I remember the blazers and ties, shiny shoes and uncomfortable nylon trousers. I remember puberty, and gladness. I remember receiving severe beatings with a belt. I remember my dick being too small. I remember sexual shyness and shame, and not knowing which was which. I remember waiting to be asked, rather than asking. I remember rejection. I remember an empty home, full of people hiding. I remember absenteeism. I remember a teacher. I remember encouragement and kindness. I remember temporariness. I remember making a decision to get my head down and work hard at school. I remember determination. I remember my exam results and the anti-climax. I remember pointlessness. I remember leaving school and looking for work."

"Wow, Kevin. I don't usually say this because I'm a therapist, so I'm supposed to know. But I don't know what to say! You've said so much."

"I don't feel well Mike. Can I go?"

"Of course Kevin. Of course."

Kevin and Mike

"Hi, Kevin."

"Hi, Mike. You ok ?"

"Not bad. You ?"

"Ok Mike. Ta"

"How have you been feeling since our last session?"

"Foggy. I feel like leaving, all the time."

"That's natural Kevin. This is a difficult place to live."

"No shit. Sorry, Mike. Don't mean to be rude."

"It's ok Kevin. Shall we continue with your life story?"

"Do we need to?"

"Not if you don't want to. I'd love to hear it though."

"Suppose so then.

"Don't Sonny boy"

"When I was sixteen years old, my mother told me that she was moving to South Africa with her new boyfriend. My sister, Natalie, was older and had moved into her own place with her husband. My other sister, Cheryl, was going with them. My mother told me that I wasn't coming. I had to stay here on my own and look after myself. She told me that I was too much trouble, and she couldn't handle it anymore. She needed a life of her own. She deserved some happiness, she said. I agreed with her. She had a hard life growing up and I was always getting into bother, in one way or other. I couldn't believe it was happening. At the same time, I pretended to her, and myself, that it was the right thing to do. I faked my understanding and acted accordingly. Until she told me that she was leaving the next day, and that the removal people were coming to pack all the stuff. I just said "Oh." I didn't show how much it hurt at the time. Until writing this, I didn't know how much it hurt at the time. I was fucking sixteen years old. I had failed miserably at school. That had nothing to do with academic ability, I just didn't go that much. So I didn't have any qualifications or a job, or any source of income. I started smoking weed about a year earlier and occasionally bought and sold some to my mates. On a good week, I could earn thirty or forty quid. That was it. I didn't know how to cook, clean, wash clothes or look after a house or flat. What the fuck was I supposed to do? The next day she was gone. She told me the council were coming to secure the house and board it up within another week. I had that amount of time to get myself sorted. In the meantime, I had some food in the cupboards and a few pieces of furniture. No telly or fuck all. I was caught between two worlds. In one, I felt sorry for my mother, and I thought that I understood her plight. In the other, I hated myself because of who and what I was. How could she leave me? I hated myself some more. After the week was up, one of my mate's uncles let me stay in a dingy little basement flat. All I had to do was give him a bit of weed now and again as payment. The flat was damp and dank. A proper shit-hole. I knew I needed a job, but I wasn't prepared to go near any of those shitty government schemes, where you work for less than fuck all at all. I read an advert somewhere about a cooking job on a boat in Ireland. I called the number, and the next day I was on a flight for the first time in my life. Right away, I loved the sensation of flying and travelling on my own. It felt like an adventure, and I was in control of it. When I got to Ireland, a huge Irish guy met me at the airport and took me to the docks. He walked, talked and looked like Hagrid from the Harry Potter films, with a broad Irish accent of course. My instincts told me not to fuck about with him. Apart from that, he was pleasant and friendly enough. At the same time, he was edgy in a lot of other ways. I told the crew on the phone that I could cook. I lied. They found out I had lied after we set sail for the Nordic coast, because I put two Fray Bentos pies in the oven with their lids on. I could have blown the galley to bits. From then on, the crew referred to me as "Fray Bentos." The captain just called me "little fucker." Every time they needed something shitty done, they said, "get Fray Bentos or Little Fucker to do it." One evening, we ran into a huge storm in the North Sea and the captain decided to set the anchor to stabilise the boat. It was a force six or seven and the boat was rocking and rolling all over the place. I was told to go out on deck and pull the handle on the big motor to release the anchor. They told me not to worry about being swept overboard because they were going to tie a rope around my waist and pull me back aboard if it went tits up. The anchor mechanism was less than fifty feet from the cabin, but it took me ten minutes to get there. Eventually, I had to crawl on my hands and knees. Those fuckers thought it was hilarious. Even more so, when I fell onto the soaking deck on the way back and they had to drag me back to the cabin on the rope. I thought my time was up. I screamed accordingly, as I slid back across the deck on my back. They never let up about it and ripped the piss out of me for the rest of the journey. My lies about cooking cost me dearly. At the end of the trip, the captain attempted to fleece the two boat owners, one being Hagrid, for the money he received for the cargo. He tried to skip through the gates of the dock in Sweden, but the owners caught him. I watched as they brought him back on board and the kicked him to bits for a good twenty minutes. I was right about Hagrid being edgy. He was more than that, because he stamped all over on the captain's body and I'm sure I heard some bones breaking. It was horrible. As soon as I got the chance, I fucked off back to my hometown. I'd made some good money from my seafaring adventures because Hagrid and the other boat owner paid me well. I think it was to shut me up about the captain's beating. They said I was good worker too.

As soon as I hit my hometown, I felt totally depressed. So, I scored a big lump of dope and jumped on the first bus to go meet a friend who had moved to a little village outside York. He went there to train as a jockey in a special school. When I got there, I pulled out the hash. Instantly, I was a big hit with my pal and his mates. They lived in the middle of nowhere and had no access to drugs. Most of them hadn't tried it before, but they all loved it. For the next few months, my life consisted of smoking dope, pissing about, and running back and forward to my hometown to score. I was making good money, had food in my belly and warm place to sleep. I was heading towards my eighteenth birthday and I didn't have a care in the world. The lads at the jockey school moved to Newmarket, so I followed right behind them. I stayed with them for another twelve months and puffed and sold dope all day, every day.

I don't know how she found me, but my mother got in touch and sked if I wanted to come to South Africa to live with her. It was a no-brainer. Of course, I wanted to go. I wanted my mother. Everyone does. When I arrived, I was shocked.

Apartheid had ended, but the place and people were still hungover from it. I couldn't stand the Afrikaans. I hated the way they talked and the tone of their accent. I found them offensive in every way. My mother was never around. I don't know why she asked me to come over. I didn't like the whole thing. After a few months, I came back home and resumed where I had left off. That's when I met Ziggy. His mam must have been a David Bowie fan. Ziggy asked me if I had ever heard of the Magic Bus. I said no. He told me about it, and its low-cost fares to Europe. He didn't have to tell me twice. At eighteen years old, I was off again on another adventure. I loved the idea of it. Within two weeks, I was dossing about in Israel. Tel Aviv, to be precise. After another two weeks, when my money had run out, Ziggy told me he had been to the British embassy to contact his mother, and she had booked him a ticket home on the next available flight. He told me he was going home, and I was on my own. Fucking great, I thought. Left to fend for myself again. I had been staying at a youth hostel for a bit, but I had to move on as my money had dwindled away. During that time, I hooked up with an older Israeli guy. He was about twenty-one. He told me to come see him if I ever needed a place to stay. So, I did. He took me to a little flat, just off the city centre. As soon as we walked through the door, he locked it behind us, pulled his trousers down, whipped out his cock and started wanking. He gestured at me to come get it. I freaked. I'm not tough and never have been, so I told him that I would jump through the second-storey window if he didn't let me go. I was serious, and he seemed to know it. He fell to his knees and started wailing at the world about how ashamed he was, and how he didn't know why he did these things. I reminded him of my high-diving intentions, so he stopped tugging and bubbling and opened the door. Twenty minutes later, I was standing in the middle of Tel Aviv without a pot to piss in and I hadn't eaten for two days. I didn't know what to do. Fuck it, I thought. I walked into the nearest hotel to scrounge some food. As I did, I spotted what looked like the manager sitting at a table covered in paperwork. I marched straight up to him and told him my story. I said that I would work for a meal. He was up for it. I spent the next two hours cleaning every toilet in the building. He kept his word and let me help myself at the buffet. Afterwards, he asked where I was staying, so I told him. Nowhere. He offered me a job and accommodation in the staff quarters, just down the road. I bit his hand off. Over the following months, I was given all of the shittiest jobs you can imagine. They treated me like a skivvy. I had nowhere else to go, so I stuck with it. I was working with the Arabs from Palestine. The Arabs built that city. They did all the mucky work and hard labour, just like me. We had a lot in common. One of the things we had in common was our love of dope. The Arabs know how to go at the stuff. Good style. The hotel manager wasn't giving me any cash for my work, but I had everything else I needed. After a few months, I did start to get paid. I was earning four hundred dollars per month. This was a lot of money to me. I swung a deal with the manager to bundle all my days-off until the end of each month. This meant that I had eight days off on-the-trot. During these times, I did what I had grown to love. I went travelling and exploring. I visited places like Jerusalem, Palestine, Haifa, Nazareth, the Dead Sea and Bethlehem, and I loved all of it. I stayed in that job for another two years. Eventually, I grew restless. One day I met a Cockney geezer. He showed me a big bag full of Lacoste shirts. Copies, of course. Back then, copies were just hitting the streets. No one had really heard of them. He told me he paid about a quid each for them in Turkey. Right there and then, I asked him to take me to Turkey to buy a thousand of them. Within four hours, we were on our way. I had plenty of cash saved up, probably four or five thousand dollars. We reached Turkey, did the deal, and jumped on train to Greece with four massive bags of hooky T-shirts. Turkish customs came on the scene, looked me and the Londoner up and down, tapped the bags and said, "What you go here?" in a broken English, half-Turkish way, "T-shirts," I told him. They forced us to open the bags. The burly Turk pushed me aside and said something in his language. I looked at him and shrugged. I had no idea what he said. Then he rubbed his thumb and forefinger together, giving me the international sign for money. He wanted a bribe. I drew one hundred dollars out my wallet and gave it to him. He looked back and gave me a big smile. "No," he said. Then he said, "Sixty to me, forty to you", and he gave me back forty dollars. When we got to the Greek border, he ushered me through the checkpoint, assured his Greek counterparts that we had been searched, and were good to go. Well, I think that's what he said. I couldn't believe my luck.

The Cockney went his own way with two hundred T-shirts. His end of the deal. I checked myself into the nearest youth hostel with the rest of the swag. The manager at the youth hostel told me that I could stay for free if I could attract customers coming into Greece at the train station, which was only five hundred yards away. That night, I brought forty-three people back with me. It was all luck. From that moment on, I was the manager's best mate. The T-shirts sold within two weeks, and my few thousand dollars tripled. I had close to ten thousand. I felt rich.

Three of the people I brought back were two Irish mandolin-playing buskers and a guy called Sten. The buskers and Sten asked me to show them around and help them out. Easy enough, I thought. From then on, I became their guide and cash collector in the streets and taverns were they played. Sten didn't do much of anything at all, but he was always there. We all played and puffed dope together and had a great time. They were all good lads, however Sten was a bit of an oddity. He was in his late thirties; a British ex-punk rocker, sporting a Mohican haircut, torn jeans and waistcoat to match. I found out later on that he was in Greece to kick a heroin habit. Apart from that, he was stark raving bonkers. He got bladdered drunk every night, and pissed in his trousers every time. More than all of that, he was a bonafide masochist. In one of his many party tricks, he would stab himself through the cheek or nose with a big darning needle. He didn't flinch, even when he was sober. So here's me, the buskers and Sten, bouncing all over Greece getting up to as much no-good as we can. As well as being a masochist, Sten was a competent fraudster. We had an Australian-Greek contact who worked in hotels and hostels across the city, and he supplied us with dodgy chequebooks, passports and American Express traveller cheques. We were raking the money in and partying hard with it. I don't know why, but Sten took a real shine to me. I think he loved me, in his own weird way. He was very protective.

I was heading out of the hostel one evening when I stopped at the top of the stairs overlooking the foyer. I stood rooted to the spot. For no apparent reason, I was overcome with absolute terror. I couldn't figure it out. At the same time, I couldn't move. After around fifteen minutes of just standing there like a dick, I summoned up the courage and determination to move. I forced myself down the stairs and past the duty worker on the desk. I walked out into the hot Greek night and felt some slight relief. That fear stayed with me for days. Looking back, I think it was a full-on panic attack. About a week later, a German guy came to stay at the hostel. He told us he had been travelling in India for a few years and he proceeded to pull out a small bag of brown powder. He told us it was heroin. Sten knew what it was before the German opened his mouth and he started shaking and sweating and telling me we were leaving. I was having none of it. I'd heard about this stuff and I was in, and up for it. Sten pleaded with me and threatened the German guy. It was no use. I could handle Sten because of our relationship. The German cooked up the heroin and put it in the syringe. I didn't need to be asked twice. I rolled up my sleeve, stuck out my arm and invited him to give me a hit. That was my first encounter with Henrietta, my pet name for heroin.

I could describe that feeling, but words don't do it justice. It's an experience that needs to be tasted. I stayed in that hostel room for about a week, until the heroin was gone. I didn't think anything of it at the time. Afterwards, we just carried on with our daily routine. Sten was never the same though. We got arrested one time for cashing stolen traveller's cheques, but I was able to talk my way out of it with the police. I don't know how I managed it, but I did it. A few weeks later, a group of us came up with the idea of scoring some more heroin. Why not, I thought. Can't-do any arm. I remembered how it had taken away all of my fears and anxiety, and then some. I wanted that feeling again. About seven of us were waiting on the heroin delivery in a café when a bunch of police came crashing in. Sten and I were singled out because we were British, I guess. There was no talking my way out of this one. These policemen were brutal-looking fuckers. And they turned to be just that. I stood at the foot of the stairs in the police station, surrounded by the thick-set thugs, and then I looked up. At the top of the stairs, an even bigger dude stood there, tapping the wall with a shortened baseball bat-looking club thing. This was it. We were getting done over for messing about with heroin in their country. Shit. They took one look at Sten and decided he was getting it first. I was a scrawny little twenty-year-old, with no meat on my bones. They hardly noticed me, in comparison to him. The guy with the bat rammed it into Sten's guts. I couldn't believe what happened next. Sten grabbed his belly and let out a big ooooooooooooooohhhhh, of pure pleasure. "That was a good one", he moaned with delight. The coppers were stunned. They thought he was taking the piss. So did I. The batter wasn't best pleased, so he gave Sten and even harder smack across his forearm. He did it again, even louder. Oooooooooohhhhh, yessss, that's the baby," he went. Slugger the Greek upped the ante and laid into Sten with a vengeance. Sten reciprocated, as any good masochist would, and rolled about the floor moaning and groaning with pure pleasure. I think he ejaculated in his Jockeys, but I can't be sure. The police threw me in a cell and returned to beating the shit out of Sten. That was the last time I saw him. When I got out, I headed back to the hostel, hooked up with the Irish buskers and got out of Dodge, sharpish. The Greek coppers had told me, in no uncertain terms, that they would kick me to bits if they ever saw me again.

Kevin and Mike

I was about 21 years old when I bolted from Greece with the Irish buskers. We caught the Euro train and headed for Italy. The buskers didn't know it, no one did, but I still had a few thousand stashed in the lining of my jacket. I vowed never to run out of money again, after the Ziggy fiasco. We were travellers, so we always met other travellers. Because of this, we knew of all the travellers' hot spots across Europe. When we arrived in Rome, we headed straight for the Spanish Steps. The place was peppered with moochers and crusty-jugglers from every country across the world. As soon as I seen it, I knew we were in the right place. The Irish lads were amazing musicians, so in less than no time at all, they were banging out the tunes and I was running around the tourists with the collection hat. Business was good. In the first few hours, we knew that cash flow wouldn't be a problem. As far as the buskers were concerned, I was an integral part of the team but I didn't feel like it. If I'm honest, I preferred flying solo. I've always been that way. When I am with people I reserve some space, just for me. They knew that I had secrets; that I visited the seedier haunts and moved around with shadier people. But they didn't mind. I might have looked OK, but I wasn't really that comfortable collecting cash with the hat. Back in Greece, when I was having a fling with Henrietta, my confidence soared and my cash collecting abilities and successes rates went through the roof. When I was caressing Henrietta and she was comforting me, everything was so much easier. But when I tried to visit her a little more often, it meant big trouble. I'm not stupid. I knew who she was. I knew she was dangerous, but that was one of the things I liked about her. I knew of her powers, and I liked those too. Henrietta and I had kissed and fooled around with some foreplay, and now I missed her. She made me feel really, really, really good. Really good.

We settled into Rome quickly. Our kind slept outdoors there, so we joined in. Why waste good money on hostel? I was slurping at a coffee one morning, on the steps, when I heard rustling in the bushes beside me. It was early and the crowds hadn't gathered yet. I took a closer look in the brush, and found a skinny Italian guy sitting with his legs crossed, injecting heroin. He wasn't skinny, so much as emaciated. He spoke some English, so we started chatting and then he showed me a big lump of hash. It was about the size of a tennis ball, and he offered it to me at a fantastic price. I bought it, and by the end of the day I had sold it on in smaller pieces to my travelling kinsmen and women. Selling dope wasn't as difficult as trying to fill the hat. Within a week, I had my own dealing-spot on the stairs and people knew where to find me. The trouble was, Bushy Bolognese was a junkie, and he was my supplier. It's a well-known fact, that him and his type are notoriously unreliable. So, for a few dollars more, or lire or euros, I can't remember which, I was able to convince him to take me to his source. His source, a Dutch guy with an unpronounceable name, offered me the same dope at half the price. Bushy was out. Now, I had a flourishing business on the go. I still hung out and helped the buskers, but it was on my terms. I preferred that. During my stint with Bushy, I eked-out the whereabouts of Henrietta's house from him. Now I knew where to find her as well. Every now and then, I'd disappear from the group and go spend some time with her. On occasion, I'd bring her back with me. And when I did, my money-making powers rocketed. In those days, I was able to take her or leave her. Fantastic lovers are hard to forget, though. Especially if they allow you to come and go as you please. Then I met Eva. Eva was a real person. She was the sixteen-year-old daughter of the British ambassador to Italy. She was all legs and tits. She looked in her twenties. That's the story I told myself anyway. Eva was fun-loving, in every way. She came from a privileged background and she wanted to rebel. I wanted to help her fulfil her ambitions. Life was great. Bouncing around Italy with a hot young babe, tons of cash and loads of hash. This went on for about nine months. Then Eva had to go, and we said our goodbyes. She wasn't naïve or vulnerable, so she didn't fall in love and start crying when we parted. Nothing like that. She knew what she wanted: a good time, and she had one. So did I.

Ever the restless adventurer, I asked the buskers and a few others if they fancied a change of scenery. It was a unanimous yes. The next day, we were off to Sardinia. What a fucking shit pit. When we got there, nearly everyone was on the gear. The travellers, the bar staff and waiters, the hotel owners and the all the vendors. You name them, they were all addicted to heroin it. One day, we went out into the countryside to find some peace and quiet to smoke a bit of dope. We found what looked like a secluded spot, just off the beaten track. But when we walked around one hundred yards, we came across thousands upon thousands of discarded hypodermic syringes. I mean thousands of them. The scene reminded me of the pictures of the killing fields in Vietnam, which are littered with human skulls. We about-turned and headed back to town. We spent four days in Sardinia, and we were sleeping on the beach. On our last morning in, we woke up and all of our stuff had disappeared. We had been robbed through the night. The buskers had tied their instruments to their wrists with the type of cord and attachment that surfers use for their surfboards. The cords had been cut and the mandolins were gone. Worse still, I had been using my jacket as a pillow and it had disappeared, along with my secret stash of cash. Somehow, the sneaky, thieving fuckers had taken it from under my head as I slept. We were in the shit. I was gutted. I had made sure that I would never run out of money. For me, this was my worst nightmare. It left me powerless, and I hated that feeling. I still hate it. I can't remember how we did it, but we scraped enough money together and made our way to Belgium. Most people say that Belgium is bland. I didn't think so. I immediately fell in love with it. For some reason, it felt like home. I still regard it that way today. We were in Antwerp, and there weren't as many travellers or tourists about. We found some cheap accommodation and some part-time work until we put enough cash together to buy some second-hand instruments. Then we worked the pubs, clubs, restaurants and streets, in the usual way. When it came to putting the hat around, the city people made me even more uncomfortable than the tourists. Cringeworthy. After getting to know a few locals, I found out that LSD was a hot commodity. You could buy it in Amsterdam and sell it in Antwerp for eight times its value. It was a Turkey T-Shirt. That's what I call a good business opportunity. I still use that phrase today and it makes me giggle every time. With deals like these, I make instinctive decisions and go for it immediately. In just about every other area of life, I'm hopeless with decisions. I try to get someone else to do the deciding for me. Usually the woman I'm with. The following day, I was on a bus and in Amsterdam in under two hours. In less than two days, I had sniffed out a dealer who was living on a barge and I was on my way back to Antwerp with an envelope full of blotting paper soaked in liquefied LSD. They were set out in little squares with a printed Om symbol. Om, as in peace brother and yoga poses. I had a go at them and found out that LSD and me don't get on that well. Far too frantic for my liking. I was permanently fearful anyway. LSD just accelerated that feeling and blew the top of my skull out. No thanks. The Antwerpians couldn't get enough of them. There's no such thing as Antwerpians. I made that up.

We were already known in the bars and clubs through busking, so the locals trusted us. Selling LSD to them was easy. Over the next few months, I settled into the city and business was a-booming again. One of our favourite clubs was a trendy joint called Het Zand. We were in that place day and night. I fell in love with a local girl and ended up living in a flat with her, just across the street from the club. I worked, played and shagged within a three-hundred-yard radius. For about year, the only time I left my circle was to jump on the train to Amsterdam and back for my supply of Oms.

We weren't the only ones living and working in Het Zand. A group of Irish guys were there more often than us. The buskers were Irish, so that made it easy to get to know them. We all ended up being friends. One particular Irish guy intrigued me. Fin, he was called. They always had plenty of money, but they didn't have jobs. My nose for the darker things in life got twitchy. I knew they were up to no good, but I couldn't pin them down. They were a tight bunch, and clammed-up quickly if anyone became too nosey. I didn't push it. One of them, Thomas, struck me as the finger-breaking type. I knew my limits. They were good enough guys, but there was no fucking around with them. We partied hard together nearly every night. One night, I noticed something familiar in Fin's expression and mannerisms. It clicked. He was on a date with Henrietta. This is a common thing amongst heroin users. You develop radar-like senses that give you the ability to spot-it-if-you've-got-it in an Antarctic white-out. Gingerly, I used winks, clicks and whistles to let Fin know that I knew and that I was interested. About an hour later, as he walked past me in the club, he reached out to me for a handshake. I reached back, we shook, and he told me to have a great night. He'd palmed me a present. Henrietta and I were back together again and we had some making-up to do. The gear was top notch, so I spent the rest of the night nodding-off in a corner. Blissful stuff.

Fin's relationship with Henrietta was a secret. His mates didn't know anything about it. They were always off their nuts on coke and booze anyway. Fin and I became good buddies after that. Now and then, we'd sneak off to an all-night bar called "In the Sweet Name of Jesus." It opened at twelve midnight, closed whenever, and it was wild. Fin and I would sit in a corner freebasing cocaine mixed with heroin for hours on end. Woopdy-fucking-doo. The place, the people in it, and the goings-on were incredible. If you could dream it up, people were doing it.

The bar was owned by a big black French guy called Jean Jack. He was up to something with Fin. They'd often disappear into a back room together for an hour so, just after we arrived. I knew not to ask any questions. I really liked Fin and I didn't want to be disrespectful or fuck up the relationship. Anyway, I was having a ball and it was none of my business. One day, Fin said that he thought I was ready to go to work. I had no idea what he meant, but I agreed with him anyway. We went to a flat in an obscure part of the city, where Fin opened up a secret compartment under a double bed. The whole thing worked hydraulically. I thought I was in a James Bond film. When the big door swung open, there must have been twenty or thirty kilos of hash in the hidden compartment underneath. He pulled out four or five big parcels and loaded them into an accordion with its innards scooped-out just for this purpose. The blocks of hash fitted perfectly. He buttoned the instrument together and nestled it in its hardened case with its maroon, velvet lining. He handed me the case and said, "see you in Norway in three days." Then he told me about the plan. He had booked train tickets for me and the buskers to travel to Oslo, along with their instruments. That was to make us look like a travelling band. He knew the buskers would listen to me, and he knew I could keep my mouth shut. I had to tell the buskers that I had sorted out a gig in Norway and it paid big money and covered all travelling expenses, including drinks and entertainment. When we got there, I had to book into a hotel and Fin would meet me there. He told me about the amounts of money involved. He paid eight hundred dollars per kilo in Amsterdam and sold it in Oslo for five thousand. Further north, in Trondheim, it fetched nearly eight thousand. That meant the contents of the accordion were worth around fifteen thousand. For a two-day journey, my end was a couple of thousand. It was a Turkey T-Shirt, size XXL.

My first drug-smuggling trip across multiple European countries was a resounding success. I had to take the drugs through the borders in Holland, Germany, Denmark, Sweden and eventually Norway. I was totally relaxed the whole time. The buskers were with me, so was Henrietta. Henrietta has the ability to make you feel invincible and invisible. In her arms, time and worry are the concerns of mere mortal men. When the deal was done, Fin travelled back separately. When I arrived back in Belgium with a wad of cash, I discovered that Fin had been arrested at the border in Germany. He was travelling on a forged passport. Instinctively, I took all of the money to his house and gave it to his wife. When Fin eventually arrived home, he told me that all of his friends had bet that I would bump him for the cash and that I would never be seen again. I've never bumped anyone in my life and I never would. I don't have that in me. That one act of loyalty cemented our relationship for life. From then on, we were a team. He was my mentor and I was his pupil. The four kilos was a trial for bigger things to come. During the next five years, Fin taught me everything he knew. He introduced me to all of his suppliers and buyers in every country across West and North-West Europe, including the UK.

The most important things Fin taught me were no powders, and stay small. He said, "never deal in powders because that is a different world with different people living in it. They will hurt you. And, stay alone and stay small. Also, don't go over the one hundred kilo mark, and don't partner-up in any deals. Keep control of your own world and keep under the radar." He drummed these rules into me all the time. I was making more money than I could spend. This was a first. I had an on-off relationship with Henrietta and believed I was in control of her. It was top of the pops for me. What an adventure! I loved every minute of it. I didn't know it at the time, but Fin had been training me to take over his business. One day, he told me he was retiring. He had made his money, bought a big farm in Ireland, and was off to spend the rest of his life with his wife, children and grandchildren to be. I know it sounds ridiculous, but there was a level of honesty and honour in our lives. We were drug smugglers, that's true, but we believed that it was only hash and there was a market for it, so why not? Fuck it. We never hurt anyone. So, here was me. European drug smuggler. You couldn't have made it up. I was the most unlikely and unassuming candidate in the world for the job. Somehow, I had the right skill-mix and attitude to carry it off.

Over the next few years, I assembled a little crew and had them running all over Europe with up to twenty kilos of Moroccans finest at a time. Sometimes more. I eventually recruited a couple of Australian travellers, who were coachbuilders back at home, to convert a mobile home and make it suitable for smuggling. When they were done, there were secret compartments all over it. They were in it, on it, under it, on top of it and down and along each side. It was an amazing piece of work by two skilled artisans. The Aussies were a couple of crustys, so I paid them in dope, beer and grub. They would have felt ecstatic about the deal, if they weren't so stoned all the time. The mobile home was perfect. It passed through all the borders hundreds of times during its reign, without ever raising suspicion. By this time, the total sum of my involvement in the smuggling included meeting the van driver in Amsterdam, paying my suppliers, saying goodbye to the driver and his cargo and waiting in the flat in Belgium for the money to arrive. My team was small and loyal. I gave everyone a good cut, every time. Back then, banks in Amsterdam never asked questions. They were, and still are, very slick with money. In total, I had close to half a million sterling stashed across three different accounts and some more hidden in and around my home.

One night, my front door flew off its hinges and landed in front of the telly. This was followed by a team of armed, uniformed police officers, dogs and detectives, all shouting and barking about something or other in their native tongue. I was in the middle of a hot and heavy session with Henrietta at the time, something that had become much more frequent. In fact, I had my own personal delivery dealer. He was a dodge-pot French-Albanian. He brought me a quarter of an ounce every time I called for it. Like money, I decided that it would be a bad idea to run out of a commodity that makes you feel so good. It made perfect sense to me. The mobile home and driver had been nabbed at the Danish border. I knew my driver hadn't given me up, but I had no idea how they had put us together. In truth, I was basking in the afterglow of an intimate encounter with Henrietta anyway. I didn't give a fuck.

Thirty-six hours later, I did give a fuck. A big one. I was in the middle of my first major heroin withdrawal and heading to prison. My alleged offence carried and compulsory one-month remand period, before going up in front of a judge. The feelings that followed reminded of the club back in Antwerp, "In the Sweet Name of Jesus." The prison was ancient. It might have been the withdrawals, but the cell felt and looked like an eighteenth-century dungeon. I half expected to see a bony guy with a beard hanging from the walls in chains. Something else that made me think of Jesus, I thought I was going to die. Instead, I puked and half shit myself to death over the next three weeks. By week four, I started to come-round and find my feet. That's when they let me out without visiting the judge. I was right. The driver hadn't given me up, and they had no evidence. I knew from then on that I was in the crosshairs of the Belgian police. They were gunning for me, and at the first opportunity, they'd shoot. I needed a plan. Right after I went to visit Henrietta, of course. I called the skinny Albanian and he delivered half an ounce, tout suite. The van driver only spent nine months in prison for over thirty kilos. I think he was released on compassionate grounds, or something. I can't recall. I decided to do a bit of travelling until all the fuss died down. I visited and called all my contacts to put the business on short-term hold, but I knew that I couldn't take too long. Market forces are powerful. Someone would fill my shoes in a matter of months. So, I fucked about a bit for a month or so and then tried to start up again. Henrietta and I were married now, and I was devoted to her. She said jump, and I said please don't leave me. I was still hustling and dealing, but it wasn't the old me. I was shoddy and careless. Looking back, I was in was full-blown heroin addiction. She had me. She promised she would one day, but I didn't listen. Too fucking smart for my own good. That's when I first noticed the raspy Scottish voice in my head. For all I know, it might have been there longer. I have no idea. It seemed to start out with the occasional criticism. Telling me how much of a tit I was for getting hooked. As time went on, the volume, content and intensity went up and up. It drove me nuts. It still does. After a month, I was back in the flat in Antwerp. One evening, the Albanian brought me two ounces on demand, but he was followed through the door by the armed response team and their canine counterparts again. He pissed himself when a gun-toting policeman jammed a submachine gun up his left nostril. The mob did the usual waving, screaming and barking affair. I was indifferent, probably wasted, maybe both. This time they had me. Two ounces of heroin in the flat, which meant it belonged to me, as far as the law was concerned. This was followed by my second serious heroin withdrawal and nine months on remand, in the same shitty, stinky jail. It took another three weeks of shitting and spewing to get over the withdrawals.

On the fourth week, I was transferred to a cell with another inmate. When I walked through the door, my new cellmate wasn't there. He was on the exercise yard. When he eventually came back, the name of Antwerp club flashed across my eyes again. This time, it was in big red neon letters. The guy was about six-foot-seven with long dark hair, a broken Roman nose and hands the size of dustbin lids. I'm sure he heard me whimper as he walked through the door. Before he arrived, I had been admiring his photos on the wall. So I gulped, hoped for the best, and asked him about them. I half expected to have my bones ground-up to make his bread. I couldn't have been further from the mark. He beamed me a big smile and started telling me about all of the people in the photos. First was his wife and kids, then he pointed to his transvestite boyfriend. He looked at me to see if was shocked, but this kind of stuff has never bothered me in the slightest. I was genuinely interested in his story and encouraged him to tell me more. So, he did. He was in prison for murder and for soliciting and prostituting underage girls. He had murdered a fortune-teller, and his transvestite boyfriend was his accomplice. They were both in the same prison. In fact, he had just been walking on the yard with him/her earlier. I didn't know whether to call his lover male or female, as she had tits and a cock. He laughed at me and told me it was OK. They murdered the fortune-teller because they went to see her one evening and they had to take along a photo of both of them for her to do her work. In the following weeks, their lives turned to shit and everything that could've gone wrong did. So one night, when they were off their heads on coke, speed and alcohol, they decided to go get the photo back. They thought the photo was at the root of their bad luck and the fortune teller has put a curse on them. When they got there, the fortune-teller refused to give them the photo, so they held her down and smothered her with a plastic carrier bag, before cutting off her head and hands. He told me the whole story without blinking. To him, it had happened, and that was that. He was just deliriously happy to have the love of his life near him, and that they were was able to walk together every day. On the yard, while walking, they were a sight to behold. They strode arm in arm and it was obvious that they were totally and utterly in love with each other. They never tried to hide it. Quite the opposite. Everyone knew their story, so no one was prepared to say a word.

The soliciting and prostituting of underage girls was harsh, as far as he was concerned. They both owned a nightclub, where they allowed prostitutes to work in exchange for a percentage of their earnings. He reckoned, that it wasn't his job to check their age and that the whole thing was a police stitch-up. Just in case the murder charge didn't stick. He wasn't sure if he would ever see the open sky again.

I ended up on remand for nine months. In the end, the Albanian admitted that the heroin was his and I walked away from a conspiracy charge for the second time. On saying goodbye to my cellmate, we both wept like children. He was one of the best friends I have ever known. I think about him often.

I walked through the prison gates a free man and headed straight to Henrietta's house. In less than twenty-four hours, I was imprisoned again, of sorts! The stint in jail had cost me about one-quarter of my cash-stash. My lawyer's fees and the judicial system in Belgium made sure of that. Robbing bastards. Just like Greece, it was time to leave town as I had a posse on my tail. I headed back to the UK with a healthy bank balance and a not-so-healthy heroin habit. Apart from some criminal drug dealer types, the only people I knew in the UK were my mates in the horse-racing scene in Haymarket. So that's where I went.

I managed to keep my head down and hide my habit for a while. Inevitably, it came on top and I had to go. They couldn't cope with that. I didn't know anything else, so I started a bit of low level dealing with some cronies I knew in Liverpool. I had all the best contacts across in Amsterdam, which were really valuable connections. I was introduced to an Irish guy. Another one! I couldn't get away from them. He was looking for large amounts of hash; one hundred kilos plus. I remembered Fin's advice and forgot it in the same breath. Fuck it, I thought. I'm bored. Amsterdam here we come.

I made the introductions and it was game on. I can't remember the Irish guy's name, and I wouldn't tell you if I did. Anyway, he told me that he was shipping the hash through the UK and then on to Ireland. I told him there was no need because I had a contact in the UK who would take the whole shipment and pay cash on delivery. It was a no-brainer for the Irish. My part of the deal was to pick up a car in London and drive it to Liverpool with the goodies on board. I was told to wait in the car and two men would load the cargo into the boot as I sat there. Then, I was told not to look at their faces, under any circumstances. I knew this was strange, but I had my head stuck in tinfoil, smoking heroin most of the time. So, it didn't register.

The day came, and I did as instructed. They weren't about to let me drive off with one hundred kilos of their hash in the boot of a car. As I was about to drive away, the passenger door opened and a heavy donkey-jacketed character landed on the seat beside me. He winked and told me, in a broad Irish accent, that I had to let the black Range Rover behind us keep in touch, all the way to Liverpool. Fuck it, I thought. I'm bored. Let's go. We stopped in Widnes and booked into a hotel. The Range rover crew disappeared. I didn't know it at the time, but the IRA had recently set off a bomb close by. It seems that the Irish crew didn't realise this either. Recent events had made the locals wary, so a skinny junkie and a burly Irishman booking into her hotel set alarm bells ringing.

While this was going on, the Liverpool contact turned up and we moved the booty from our car to his. He drove off to Liverpool to check that the hash was legit, and he would call us to come collect the money when he was satisfied. I turned to big Irish and asked him if he trusted the Scouser. He said that it didn't matter because they would kidnap his children if he tried any funny business. I remembered Fin's rules and forgot them again because it was time to hit the toilet and have a chat with Henrietta. As I was sitting on the bog having a boot, the door came in, just like Belgium, and armed police officers swarmed the place. Once again, I was on the ground with a gun behind my head. Henrietta intervened, so I didn't register the feelings.

When we got to the cop shop, the heavy hitters came to interview me. They're easy to spot. They're just as bad as the people they chase. I suppose they need to be. No point asking a mouse to chase a cat. The team leader took one look at me and said, "Why the fuck is someone like YOU, associated with someone like HIM?" I shrugged and acted all innocent. Then he said "I've missed something with you two, I know it. Somethings happened, and I've just missed it. You two don't belong in the same scene. You need to stay clear of these guys. You won't last and you don't want to know what they do for kicks." I was right. He was just like the people he chases. Hardened criminals just know. They have a nose for it. So did he, and he didn't doubt his instincts for a second. Me and big Irish were bundled in a car, driven out of town and told never to come back. This pattern was becoming tedious. I needed a change. When the hash deal was done, I remembered Fin's rules for the third time, and I listened. I knew I was way out of my depth with these guys. They asked me for two hundred kilos next time. I gave away the Amsterdam contact for free and booked a flight for South Africa.

Kevin and Mike

I booked the next available flight to South Africa via Amsterdam, which left in two weeks' time. I could have flown directly from the UK quicker, but Henrietta and I were getting a divorce. This was it. I was leaving her for good this time. I hated the fucking bitch and I loved the fucking bitch. She had robbed me of my dignity, my self-respect, my earning powers and most of my health. I knew she was after my money too, and I knew she wouldn't be happy until it was all gone. Fuck that, I thought. No way. I vowed never to be in that position again. I couldn't bear another Sardinian adventure. I was serious about kicking her, so I needed a detox pack to get me through the flight and the withdrawals when I got to South Africa. I knew Amsterdam like the back of my hand, and I knew who had what and how to get it. So, I arranged the medicines I needed by phone and I intended to grab them during the stop-over leg of the flight. While I was waiting for my flight, I dodged around Liverpool for a bit. Scoring heroin and crack wasn't that difficult there. After all, I needed to do something to pass the time. I was bored. Always on the lookout for a Turkey T-shirt, I happened to bump into a couple of old acquaintances who were manufacturing and selling designer clocks. They were brothers. The clock bodies they were making were really nice. To make them, they poured different colours of liquid resin into pre-shaped moulds. It was a simple process. They looked like ornate, marble, art-deco type things. The clock mechanisms were just cheap Chinese shite. Nevertheless, they only cost one pound fifty to make and sold for a tenner, all day long. Right up my street. I couldn't resist it. In a flash, a plan came together and a deal was done. We agreed that one of the brothers would come to South Africa with me to set up shop. He wanted to get off the gear too. As part of the deal, I was supposed to help him out by sharing my detox meds. We were going international. Detoxing Clock Makers Inc. We would transport the manufacturing kit and moulds out ahead of us, which was handy for me because I was able to stash my detox pack in amongst it. Minus what I needed for the flight, of course. I must have bought about a year's supply of heroin substitute tablets and Valium. The tablets alone filled a small suitcase. As ever, I thought that running out of the stuff that makes you feel good was a fool's game. After all, drugs and money were my favourite feel-good things. Next stop, Durban, South Africa.

Looking back, heading for Durban seemed like a good idea at the time because the European and British police were up my arse, and I wanted to get clean. But, I could have gone anywhere. I think I might have been chasing after my mother. After all, I'm sure everyone needs a mother's love when they're fucked. Don't they? I don't know. I'm not sure why I went there. Anyhow, the plan worked and we set up a little factory in Durban as soon as we got there. I put my detox on hold and kept taking the substitute meds. We started making the clocks and I hit the road on a sales mission. I had plenty of tablets to keep me going and I had no intention of rekindling my love-hate relationship with Henrietta. Before long, business was a-booming. Again. The gift shops and supermarkets all across Durban couldn't get enough of the stuff. I was constantly on the go and making money. I thought I was happy enough.

My Liverpudlian business partner was getting right on my tits. One minute he was thrashing around a scabby flat in Durban, withdrawing from heroin. Two minutes later, he was wearing a French beret and pretending to be an Artisan Craftsman, while cavorting with a bunch of other pretentious arty-type twats. I needed shot of him. One day, I met this Australian fella and I showed him our little business set up. He fell in love with it and immediately offered us nearly two hundred thousand Rand for the moulds alone. The exchange rate didn't matter. That was enough money to buy a good-sized house. But, I couldn't convince Van Gough to take the deal. The moulds were his really, so I was stuck with them, and him. Round and around I went. As far as I knew, Henrietta wasn't popular in this part of the world. That's one of the reasons I went there. How wrong was I. After Apartheid, Nigerian gangs flooded the country, and they brought Henrietta and her cousin Katy crack pipe with them. One day, while selling my wares in Johannesburg city centre, I met a kindly, beautiful, big bosomed, black female. I knew she was kind because she offered me a big ball of crack cocaine and a good time for fifty Rand. I'd never seen anything like it. The crack ball was the size of a jaw-breaking gobstopper. Only much more shiny-white and sparkly. The exchange rate suddenly mattered again. Fifty Rand was about five pounds sterling. In the UK, the crack ball would have cost a couple of hundred quid, easy. I was bored. Why not, I thought. I didn't want to be rude to the nice young lady. After a three-day crack binge with my new black friend, I was lying on her bed with a spangled brain and a red-raw penis, when a visitor came a-knocking. It was Henrietta. She had found me. Only this time, she was stronger, cheaper and more bountiful. The Nigerian gangs made sure of that.

Henrietta and I were in the throes of it again. It was the same as all the other times, apart from the quality, quantity, price and availability of her touch. I got really greedy with her this time. It was hard not to. I was barely pissing about with the clock business, so that money started to dry up. The Scouser couldn't cope with the situation, so he fucked off home. I was left with the moulds and the business. I still had my secret bank accounts too. As soon as he boarded the plane, I moved the whole kit and caboodle to Johannesburg. I rented a little garage with a flat above it, in a place called Hillbrow. I didn't know it at the time, but Hillbrow was, and still is, one of the most dangerous places in Johannesburg. I told myself that it was a strategically sound business decision. But really, I was moving closer to my drug suppliers. In under a month, my drug habit rocketed as the business plummeted. While I was dicking about in Hillbrow, I bumped into a fella called Jason from Manchester. I can't forget him, no matter how hard I try. Jason was like an imaginary accident. He makes me cringe every time he enters my thoughts. He still does today. He was by far, the slipperiest, most conniving, dangerous man I have ever had the displeasure of knowing. I nicknamed him the Machiavellian Mank. Not that I ever said that in front of him. He was only in the country for six months, and somehow he had mastered the Nigerian language, become a police informer and was running a team drug mules back and forward from Thailand. He fucked and double-crossed everybody, all the time. Even the police. I moved about with him for a bit, because we did the drugs together and we were both British in a foreign country. Then he set me up in a stupid little drug deal and I came close to ending up in a ditch with my hair on fire. I couldn't get rid of him quickly enough. I can't imagine he survived for that long. He was totally fearless and utterly ruthless. Or, maybe he was just mad and bad. Probably all of the above. For the next year, I circled the drain. Every now and then, I would convince myself that I was ready to quit. Then, I would drive for twenty-four hours to Cape Town, promising to make a fresh start. I didn't take any drugs with me. As soon as I arrived, the voice in my head went mental. So, I about-turned and drove straight back to Johannesburg. As soon as I got back, I scored more drugs. I must've made that trip twenty times. One hot, sticky night, I was marching back from my dealers in Hillbrow and the police stopped me. They searched me and found a bag of heroin. I thought nothing of it at the time. On the streets of Hillbrow, murder was the norm. So at worst, I thought I could bribe them with a few Rand and be on my way with a slapped wrist. Not so. A Brit buying and using heroin in their fair country was a big slur. Woosh. Off I went, up in front of a tutting judge who sent me to Diepkloof prison for the insult.

Now, money didn't concern me and I had been using copious amounts of heroin and crack cocaine every day for over a year. All of a sudden, I'm in the middle of a crashing comedown and heading to Hades. Diepkloof was, and is, the dumping ground for South Africa's worst of the worst. Think of the prison set up in the old film, Midnight Express. Double it and don't flush the toilet for a couple of months, then you'll begin to imagine what Diepkloof is like. There were twelve big cells in the joint, with sixty people to a cell. Each cell was run and managed by the Numbers gangs. The guards were bystanders, at best. Everything had to be paid for in cash. Food, toilet roll, clothing, visits and tobacco. Everything. Ninety percent of the inmates were murderers. The rest were murderers and rapists. One of the guards was Irish. What was it with Irish people and me? He took one look at me and said, "what the fuck are you doing in here? I hope you make it kid, but judging by the way you look, I doubt you will. Take some advice. Don't get sick. Sick people don't recover in here." Then he shook his head and walked off. I didn't see him again. I often wonder if I was delusional or if I just dreamt about him. After all, I was shaking and shitting myself to death, without any arse wiping implements or soap and water.

I spent the first three nights in the toilet. Not because I was shitting muddy pond water. One of the gang captains ordered me to sleep there. I wasn't allowed in the main cell. Eventually, I convinced him that I was getting a visit soon and money was on its way. I promised to pay him if he let me in the main cell and found me some food. Reluctantly, he agreed. It wasn't out of pity. Like every other emotion, that one was redundant in there. For the next two weeks, I lay in my own piss, shit and muck until the withdrawals subsided a little. No one took any notice of me. I had nothing for anyone. When I raised my fuzzy head above the parapet, I noticed a small curtained-off square in the middle of the cellblock. It looked strangely out of place. Without thought, I walked over and looked behind it. All at once, four or five gang members grabbed me and started shouting all sorts of obscenities in fragmented Afrikaans. I thought my time was up. The gang leader who ran the cell lived behind the curtain, and it was a punishable offence do what I had just done. There were two punishment options available. I could be stabbed to death, or shagged up the arse and then stabbed to death. When the numbers gang rape men for punishment, they make you lie face up so they can watch your expression. I don't think they're interested in eye to eye passion. For the umpteenth time in my life, I was saved by the bell. In this case, the bell happened to be the gang leader. I was the only white Brit in the jail, which seemed to interest him. When I first seen him, he reminded me of Idi Amin. I was hoping he had a better temperament. He beckoned me forward and told me to sit. I dropped my arse quicker than an obedient dog. Firstly, it was to please him. Secondly, I was trying to hide it from the overeager punishment squad. I couldn't believe my luck. It turned out that Idi loved horseracing. Jackpot. I had lived and breathed horseracing for years with my Aintree posse. Right away, I started name-dropping all the best trainers and jockeys in the UK and the ones in his country. He knew his eggs. He was well impressed with my knowledge, and even more so when we began to talk betting and race fixing. He loved to gamble and he loved cheating even more. I won a reprieve. He gave me a bed-like-thing and told someone to feed me. For the next couple of weeks, we were best buddies. The gang captain that I had promised money was pestering me about it. Idi told me that he had to respect his captains, so he couldn't side with me. I wasn't really due a visit or any money. It was a blag. Ding Ding. Round two. I was getting moved to one of the less salubrious cells for lying. The one I was in was at the top of the comfort scale but as you moved down the order, they got progressively worse. I thought they were joking. It couldn't possibly get any worse. But it did. By miles. I was moved two cells down and I shit myself again. This time it was inspired by fear, not the withdrawals. My new cellmates were hardly human. Every one of them was covered from head to toe in fleas as big as rats, and they constantly scratched and clawed at themselves. I remembered the Irish guard's warning: "Don't get sick in here". Now I knew why he said it. There was even a group of them shagging each other in a corner of the cell. No one had any money. When feeding time arrived, the guards delivered a big cauldron of greenish stuff and it was every man for himself. I remember having to hold my nose to stop gagging whenever I ate it, otherwise I would have starved. Looking back, I'm amazed at how I adapted and survived in that environment. After another couple of weeks, one of the guards came to the cell and told me I had been bailed. Halleluiah Amen, I thought. I now knew why people liked to have a God in their lives. The guard whipped me to reception for release but when we got there, I was turned around and sent back. I couldn't believe it. I can't describe my feelings as I was marched back to the cell that day. Expressions such as gutted, disappointed and bereft don't do them justice. The guards told me that news of my imprisonment in Diepkloof had reached some friends, and they had sent ten thousand Rand by courier to bail me out. It turned out that the Numbers gangs caught wind of the money as it was on its way to the jail, so they tried to rob the courier outside the prison. He managed to escape them, and the bail money eventually reached me a few days later. The courier was a friend of a friend. As I walked through the reception doors, his smiling face turned yellowish white and he promptly vomited all over his own feet. When I eventually put myself in front of a mirror, I understood why. I was the spitting image of Smeagol from Lord of the Rings. And I smelled like him too. For nine weeks, I hadn't washed, changed my clothes or eaten anything substantial. On top of that, I had pissed, spewed and shit myself through the worst withdrawals of my life. I needed Henrietta, and the courier hadn't brought her along to meet me. I cursed him for it, then made him drive me straight to Hillbrow. I scored some gear, sorted myself out, locked up the workshop, put the moulds in storage, scored some more gear and headed to my mother's in Durban for some R&R. When I got there, her reception was cold. After a few weeks, she told me she was heading back to the UK because I was too much for her. Fuck it, I thought. I'm going to Cape Town. So I did. I gathered up the remainder of my detox meds, headed to Cape Town, stayed this time, detoxed myself and started all over again. Again. That's when I met the Cash Crusaders. The Cash Crusaders were a couple of Aussie-African entrepreneurs. On a recent holiday back in the land of Kangaroos and Koalas, they came across the Cash Converters chain and decided to replicate the business model in South Africa. They called it Cash Crusaders, for copyright reasons. Anyhow. Their family were already rich, so they managed to set it up and roll out a franchise model within a few months. I teamed up with an Indian businessman and took on one of the franchises. It lasted about six months. The Indian was a depressive hypochondriac. He was in his bed more often than not, and I was left to run the business. I pulled out of the deal and lost a fair chunk of money, but I was richer for the experience. Now, I knew how to operate a pawnbroker shop. So, I opened one of my own. What else was I going to do? I was bored. The South Africans love trading in gold and diamonds. Because of this, I was moving hundreds of ounces of gold every week within the first few months. It was simple. I paid, say, one hundred Rand per ounce and sold it for two hundred. Like any other pawnshop, I would also lend money against gold as collateral. If the customer didn't pay back the loan within the allotted time, I sold it. As soon as a customer gave me some gold, I had it provisionally sold within the hour at a set price. Most of the people who came into the shop were either desperate or the goods were stolen. Legally, all I had to do was photocopy their ID's. Most of which was fake anyway. Business was-a-booming. Again. And again, I got bored. I missed Henrietta so much. Life just wasn't the same without her. It wasn't quite the same with her either, but the bad times are easily forgotten. A love like that, always seems worth another shot. Pardon the pun. I couldn't resist her and within a month, I had a raging habit once more. The money was flying in and flying back out just as quick. I would open up at nine in the morning, make my first few hundred Rand, close the shop for an hour, go see my dealer, smoke a big crack ball, shoot some heroin to counteract the effects of the crack, then go back to the shop for the rest of the day. It was a good system, but it was destined to fail. Drug habits always spiral upwards. Exponential growth and greed is guaranteed. One day, I met a guy, who knew a guy, who heard about a guy growing the best weed in South Africa. My ears pricked up at the sound. I pulled on the thread of those rumours, and I eventually found out who this guy was and how to get myself an introduction. Selling weed was familiar territory. I knew how to find my way around this land without raising suspicion. To cut a long story short, I ended up finagling a deal to smuggle loads of weed back to Western Europe. The rumours were right. It was the best weed I had ever tried, and it was a cheap as chips. I re-ignited my old contacts in Amsterdam and away we went. Now I was wasn't as bored, so I eased up on the hard drugs a bit and went back to work. It excited me.

Meanwhile, I left the pawnshop in a semi-friends incapable hands. I didn't really care. I was giddy at the thought visiting my old stomping ground in Europe. The best weed grower in South Africa wasn't the type to be trifled with. I'd met his kind before, and I knew I needed to be careful. The first few deals went without a hitch, so I relaxed and started taking Henrietta along for the ride. That's when I lost about twenty thousand pounds in cash in a coffee shop in Amsterdam. I had stuffed the money in a woolly sock and stuffed that inside my jacket. Thinking only of Henrietta, I left the jacket on the seat and I went to the toilet for a kiss with my lover. I didn't notice the sock had gone until I boarded the flight to South Africa. When I felt for the money, and it wasn't there, eight units of blood fell straight to my feet. I knew that I was chalk white because I felt that way. The plane shot down the runway, and that was that. At thirty thousand feet, I remembered a slippery little Moroccan twat in the coffee shop. He was sitting far too close and paying far too much attention. He must've watched me go to the toilet, then relieved me of the sock in my jacket. Merry Christmas for him. When I got back to South Africa, I told the best weed grower in South Africa what had happened. He wasn't interested and gave me four hours to get his money. I still had plenty of cash stashed in the bank, so I reluctantly obliged. He didn't take kindly to my reluctance. For reputation's sake, he needed to let me know who he was. A week later, he lured me into a meeting with a couple of heavy hitting Aryan brother types and they tried to take me for a little ride in their car. One of them told me not to run before he opened the car door. Then, he opened his coat to let me see his gun. As soon as he opened the car door, I ran. As I was running, I tried to pull my head my down into my torso and scrunched my face up, waiting for the bang. I reached the end of the street and a cop car pulled up. Its occupants asked me why I was running. I gave them some lame excuse and looked over my shoulder to see my would-be lesson-teachers drive off. I've never been so glad to see the police. That was the end of that.

I went back to the pawnshop and carried on where I had left off. Eventually, the drugs took their toll and I needed to flee the scene of the accident. As usual, I thought moving countries would solve my problem. It's called the geographical shuffle. This time I headed back to the UK.

When I got there, I headed to Newmarket to hook with the people I knew in horseracing. I visited my mother first. Her reception was cold. I'm still not sure if I was following her, but a familiar pattern was emerging.

The horse racing fraternity humoured me for a while. They liked me well enough, but they just couldn't take the idea of me and the hard drugs scene. Who can blame them? I tried to sort myself out but fucked it up as usual. Also, I wasn't earning and started to notice big holes appearing in my bank accounts. Just as I was about to be ousted by the horsey folks, one of them asked me if I wanted to go with him to work on a film set to train horses. And you'll never guess where? South Africa, of all places. If I wanted to go. I needed to get clean. There was no way around it. Fuck it, I thought. I'm bored. I'd never worked on a film set before. It might be good. So, I locked myself up in a hotel for a few weeks and sweated, spewed and skitter-shitted all the poison out of my system. Again.

I had my sights set on Hollywood. It was the big time for me from now on. But, chronic depression had a different agenda. I got clean, headed back to South Africa, got a job as a runner on the set of a film called "Racing Stripes" and promptly fell into the darkest and deepest moods I have ever known. I couldn't even muster the energy to think about killing myself. It would have been too much effort. The movie makers weren't interested in my plight. They fucked me off in a heartbeat. The film was shite anyway. So here's me, banged up in a scummy hostel, deeply depressed and unable to string a sentence together. I could've afforded a hotel, but I was tightening my belt. I was down to my last twenty or thirty thousand.

I was sitting downstairs in the hostel canteen one day, trying to force down some scrambled eggs, when Mr Pedro François De-Beer approached me. Pedro had a Spanish, French and Dutch name. He was gregariously gay; a skilled con man and a shameless rent boy. What a character. As soon as I met him, I cheered up. It was hard not to. He had boundless energy and enthusiasm for life, and he lived it very fast indeed. He told me he had been watching me for about a week and he knew that I was in a dark place. As far as he was concerned, it was his duty to pull me from my slump.

Over the next few months, Pedro and I travelled to all the South African hot spots and had a wail-of-a-time. One day, he told me that he used to manage a fashion magazine and he thought that we would be able to set one up in Cape Town. He reckoned we could make good money from it. I still wasn't earning, so I agreed. He laid out the plan. We would advertise for candidates to attend an interview and photo shoot in a top hotel. The advert would say that we were looking for a model to become "the face" of the magazine. He would be the front man, while I would occupy the background as a British investor. This was partially true, as I had thrown in a few thousand to get the thing rolling. I had my doubts about the scheme, but Pedro seemed to know what he was doing. I had no reason not to trust him. He set the whole thing up within four weeks. He was as smooth as warm butter. On the day of the interviews and photos shoot, over one hundred fame seekers turned up for their chance to shine. To make my role more plausible, I wore a cream cotton suit and a Panama hat while I sat in plain sight of the interviewees. Pedro did his thing and the interviews lasted for three days. On the fourth day, the hotel manager came to my room and told me that a crowd of people were at reception waiting for me. I had no idea what he was on about. I got dressed and knocked on Pedro's door to tell him about the manager's concerns. No answer. I tried calling him. No answer. I went down to the lobby and was met by an angry crowd who claimed I owed them lots of money. It clicked. Pedro had swindled all of us. It turned out that he had taken deposits from all of the interviewees and promised to provide every one of them with glossy portfolios and secondary interviews. He left every one of them with the idea that they were in with a chance of becoming famous and that I would make it happen for them. During the interviews, he had pointed them towards me as I sat in the background and told them that I was the big cheese. I was in trouble. Again. The crowd were getting angrier by the minute, especially since I had told them that I didn't have their money. For my safety, the hotel manager called the police and off I went to the cells.

As far as the police were concerned, I was just as guilty as Pedro. It didn't matter what I said, they were having none of it. Neither was the judge, who sent me straight to prison on remand. This time, it was Westville prison in Durban. I wasn't withdrawing from hard drugs and I wasn't suffering the way I did in Diepkloof. Westville wasn't bad as Diepkloof either, but it was still a shit hole and I was still the only white Brit in the place. It took me four weeks to get word to the same friends who bailed me out last time. They arrived early one Saturday morning to pick me up, and again the relief was indescribable. On the drive back to Cape Town, we pulled into a service station for food and fuel. I looked across the forecourt and noticed a familiar figure standing at the station entrance. He seemed to be thumbing a lift. I could not believe my eyes. It was none other than Pedro, Francois De-Beers himself. "Oi, you cunt," I shouted, and sprinted across the concrete road towards him. When I got there, I grabbed him and raggy-dolled him up and down the street while screaming in his right ear about betrayal and friendship, and all that. I don't know why I didn't punch his face in. I think I was still holding some gratitude because he rescued me from my depression and potential suicide. My bail bearing liberators caught sight and sound of the commotion and came over to pull me off him. I told them the story and we agreed that the best course of action would be handing him to the police. So, we did just that. On hearing the story, the police arrested both of us and put us up in front of the same judge who sent us back to the same prison that I had been released from two hours earlier. Looking back, I should have seen the signs. My luck had been running out for some time. I was on a slippery slope. After four weeks, an initial hearing was scheduled and Pedro and I were summoned to the prison reception to catch a bus to court. After waiting for a few hours, the guards took me back to the cell because no one could find Pedro. Somehow, he had disappeared inside the prison. The same thing happened another three times. On the fourth time, my lawyer told me that if Pedro didn't turn up for the hearing five times, then I would be set free and all charges would be dropped. It was something to do with South African law. That day came, and Pedro failed to materialise. The judicial system had no alternative. They had to set me free and drop all the charges as promised. To this day, I still don't know what happened to Pedro. I guess he knew how the legal system worked and somehow managed to hide from it in plain sight. On the other hand, he might have been killed and eaten. Nothing could surprise me about South African prisons.

After that, I lost the stomach for Turkey-T shirts and any other kind of shady dealings. My arse had fallen out, as they say. I headed back to Johannesburg and resigned myself to Henrietta's allure. My love for her was all-powerful. There was nothing I could do. I had lost my ability to resist her. For the next two years, I whittled away at the remainder of my cash-stash without replenishing it. Most of it went into my arm and lungs. The rest of it disappeared through a series of bad deals and bad judgment calls. I was also robbed from time to time. After all, I lived and moved about in Hillbrow. That's when I got stabbed in the neck by a couple of muggers. Now I'm here.

"You've been about a bit Kevin."

"I know Mike. I was there."

Kevin and Mike

"Hi, Kevin. Thanks for attending the session today. How are you feeling?"

"OK-ish . Cheers. How are you?"

"I'm fine. Thanks for asking. How did you feel after telling me your life story last week?"

"Relieved. It was good to spit it all out. Are you going to report me to the courts for non-participation in the programme?"

"No Kevin. But I need you to do me a favour."

"What?"

"Don't tell any of the other residents that you didn't write your life story. They'll start shouting about discrimination and favouritism. Can you do that?"

"Of course. I don't talk to many of them anyway. Trust issues, and all that. You know what I'm like."

"I'm starting to get to know what you're like Kevin. I enjoy talking with you."

"Me too Mike. Me too."

"As you know Kevin, we use the Twelve Step programme to help people overcome their addiction problems. We spoke about it in previous sessions and you seemed resistant to the concept. What are your thoughts on it today?"

"I've been reading the literature and attending some meetings, Mike. There are some parts of it that appeal to me and there are others that don't."

"Do you want to tell me about it?"

"Sure. I think the abstinence concept makes perfect sense. I've been using and abusing drugs and alcohol for years and years and I've never been able to maintain control over them. Well I have on occasions, but eventually I always end up chronically addicted in one way or another. So for me, staying clear of them all together will guarantee that I won't end up back in the same hole. I like that idea. I don't know why I didn't think of it before. I also like the parts where it asks you to reflect on the past and take personal responsibility for your actions. I also like the parts where it encourages personal development in the present and the future. However, I'm not so keen on the religious connotations or some of the other concepts and doctrines. I don't agree with the idea that addiction is a disease. Overall, I think the whole things is riddled with cultish ideologies."

"Cultish? That's a bit it strong Kevin. What do you mean?"

"Well, the Twelve Step literature implies that addiction is an incurable disease and that relapse is inevitable unless the Twelve Step programme is followed . I don't think that's fair. If I was vulnerable and susceptible to suggestion, and if my life depended on it, I could be fooled into believing that this was true."

"This is our experience, Kevin. There are hundreds of thousands of people across the world who use the Twelve Step programme, and they say the same thing."

"Why? What's in it for them?"

"That sounds cynical Kevin?"

"I suppose it does. But the question still stands. In my opinion, offering-up such a powerful fait accompli to vulnerable people is nothing short of cultish behaviour. Like I said. There's another thing. I don't know how someone as intelligent as you can't see or doesn't agree with this? Surely you know that an organisation is putting its own needs before its members if encourages them to believe in such a dogmatic system. Especially if those members are vulnerable and hopeless. The churches used the same strategy. Although the churches were even more perverse because they created the vulnerability and hopelessness, to begin with. Do you see where I'm coming from Mike? Or not?"

"For someone who has been addicted to drugs for most of his adult life Kevin, that's a powerful and profound insight."

"Are you surprised? Did you think that addiction and intelligence were mutually exclusive? For someone who has worked with addicts and alcoholics for so many years Mike, that's profoundly short-sighted and closed-minded. If that's what you think, of course."

"That's not what I meant Kevin. I feel as if you're being antagonistic and sarcastic. Are you?"

"No. Do you feel offended?

"No. No-one has ever put it to me in that way before. If anything, I feel challenged. But I understand why. What do you think of the amends process in the Twelve Steps? What do you know about it?"

"Only what I've read and heard."

"Ok. What's that then?"

"I've read and heard that it's about making amends to people that I've harmed."

"Yes. That's it really. What do you think of it?"

"Can't-do any harm!"

"Very witty Kevin. Seriously. What do you think or it?"

"I'm not so keen."

"Why's that?"

"Isn't it obvious? Who would want to do that? All I've ever done is look after number one. I've never been that bothered about other people. To be honest, I'd rather move on and forget about it."

"What about your family?"

"What about them?"

"Your mother and sisters. Wouldn't you like to re-establish contact with them?"

"Why do you ask that Mike?"

"Because I think it's important? I think it would do you some good to see them. I think it would be good for them as well. If you're serious about recovering from your addiction problems Kevin, it will help you to heal the past"

"Do you think I'm not serious?"

"You seem so, but you never know. I've seen this before. All of a sudden people change their minds and go back to their old lives. I wouldn't like to second guess you. Just in case. You know?"

"Yeah. Given my track record, I wouldn't bet on me either. I know I seem a bit arrogant and aggressive at times Mike, but I do want to sort this shit out."

"Ok then. I would like to arrange for your family to visit you here for a conversation. Are you up for it?"

"No. But I'll do it anyway."

"Good. I'm glad. I'll make the arrangements. In the meantime, can you have a think about how your behaviour has harmed your family? Either directly or indirectly. I'd ask you to write it all down but I'm guessing you won't.

"You're right Mike. I won't. I'd rather say my piece when I see them. I know what I've done. I don't need to write about it."

IS THIS TRUE ?

Brutus, Cheryl and Eileen

What's that smell?

We're going on a day out. Woof Woof. Can't wait. This is gonna be priceless. I listened to Chez telling Oslo that her brother Kevin had reappeared on the scene. I've only ever heard his name mentioned a few times. If I was inclined to believe the hype, which I'm not, then Kevin is responsible for most of this fucked-up family's woes. When the wooden tops, Chez and Eileen, rub heads together, they revel in recounting each and every one of Kevin's evil deeds. The thing is, he doesn't sound that evil to me. But when those two are having a go at him, they make him sound like the devil incarnate. Apparently, he's in rehab. Chez said that one of the counsellors had contacted Eileen and asked if she would consider visiting him so that he could apologise for all the shit and disruption he has caused over the years. Eileen agreed to go and Chez agreed to ride shotgun. I had no choice in the matter. I was going, whether I liked it or not. Just before we set off in the car, Chez took me for a quick walk and told me that I needed to take a piss and shit before the journey started. The daft munter thinks she's Pavlov. She doesn't use a bell in her attempts to control me though. She uses a complete personality change. It's fucking weird. I think it's her primary school teacher persona. "Now Brutus!" she says, in a voice and tone known only to that type, "Cheryl and mummy are taking you in the car and you need to go poo-poo and pee-pee before we set off. There's a good boy, you can do it if you try." What's the deal with primary school teachers anyway? What are those fuckers up too? That's one weird bunch of human beings. In fact, all human beings are weird, but that lot are especially so. Whatever would make them want to take up a job like that? I think they belong in the same category as police and prison officers. Why would anyone want to take control over a bunch of people who don't want to be controlled? Criminals and young kids want to do whatever they like and they don't really care about the consequences. They need to ask themselves some serious questions. I took up the offer of a piss, but no shit though. I held that one in and I'm baking it for badness. I'll be sitting on Chez's lap for the whole journey. When the fermentation process is complete, I'll drop a couple of silent and deadly numbers for Eileen while she's driving. I'll be staring right at her when I let one go. I've recently mastered smiling too, so I'll flash my gnashers at her as well. Any backchat from the bitch and she'll be needing another trip to the nail salon. Anyway, we're off on the four-hour car journey now. This rehab reunion will be the stuff of legend. I'm sure of it.

Brutus, Cheryl, Eileen, Kevin and Mike

What's that smell?

Here we go. We've arrived at the rehab and we're waiting for Kevin and his counsellor to enter the fray. Cheryl's fidgety. Eileen is ice-cold-calm. I've never seen another human being with her capacity and skill. She just does not give a fuck about anyone else apart from herself. She is, undoubtedly, the best person on the planet at being an absolute cunt. No doubt about it. Right. They're here. The show is about to begin.

Kevin's looking healthy. That's a new one. There's an older guy with him. He must be the counsellor. Bit of a podgy-yet-solid dude with most of his teeth missing. That gummy smile doesn't seem bother him in the slightest though. He's got a right old swagger about him. It's obvious that he'll be conducting this orchestra. He doesn't know it yet, but Eileen will try to steal his baton as soon as a gap in the music appears. As they both sit down, Kevin shoots a quick look in Eileen's direction. It's definitely not one that speaks of gladness at a mother and son's reunion. It's something altogether different. I can't decipher it. Next, he flashes a glance in Cheryl's direction. This one's simple enough to read. It's pity. He leans over and scratches behind my ear. I fart. Partly, it's an appreciative response to Kevin's touch. On the other hand, I cant be letting Eileen and Mike compete for all the thunder in the room. It fucking stinks and Kevin's the only one to laugh. Mike's trying his best not to, and I'm hoping that he fails. Cheryl's post box red with embarrassment, because of her attachment issues to me, and I'm sure that the Kevin's counsellors training kicks in because it looks as if he makes a mental note of it. Eileen treats the event and the arrival of the aroma with utter disdain by pretending to ignore it, and me. I stare straight at her, and fart again. The first one was only just hearable, but the follow-up has a bit of pressure behind it, so it's impressively noisy. Kevin falls apart, Cheryl goes redder and the counsellor guy stiffens his resolve and holds his composure. Impressive. Eileen's top lip curls up on the right hand side, just like Elvis. I kept staring at her, half-smiling, half-growling. Kevin dives deeper into his hysteria. It would be easy to assume that nervousness was the driving force behind his guffawing, but it looks and feels like genuine amusement. I knew this was gonna be a good day. Mike steps in and tries to rescue the situation. "Good afternoon everyone. My name's Mike. I'm Kevin's primary counsellor and I'll be guiding us through the process today. It's nice to see you both. I'll just open a window for a second. Must be the long journey. Dogs don't travel well." They all wait for a minute or so, while Kevin pulls himself around. Mike hands him a disposable tissue from a box that he brought in with him. I bet he never expected using them to mop up tears of laughter. Eileen clocks Mike's obvious stature, power and control over his emotions. In response, she rolls her shoulder back and rears-up for the tussle. Mike notes that one too. "Hello Michael. I'm Eileen, Kevin's MOTHER, and this is his sister, Cheryl." The white in Cheryl's eyes shine out from behind her big red beamer. All she manages is a limp-ish "Hi……I'm Cheryl…..Hi…..cough, cough ahemm!". Mike continues in the lead, and acts as if he missed the tone and intent behind Eileen's use of his full forename. I'm beginning to like him. He's cucumber-cool; a potential ally. "Hi Eileen. Hi Cheryl. Thanks for attending the session today to help Kevin with his recovery." Cheryl and Eileen react in synchronistic bitterness, with a well-rehearsed, "Hmmphh." The idea that Mike thinks they travelled all this way to talk about Kevin and HIS wellbeing has them looking straight at each other in a manner that suggests they think he's a bit nutty and confused. Mike notes that one as well. At the same time, he notes that he is making far too many notes so early in the game. He raises one eyebrow, unlike Elvis's lip, and for the briefest moment, he seems perplexed at Eileen and Cheryl's behaviour. Quickly, he gathers himself and asks, "What's the little dog's name?" Under her breath, Eileen mutters, "rotten arse." I bark and snarl and yearn for the taste of nail varnish. Cheryl woke up. "Mum! Don't." Eileen takes the hint and backs off. She knows that Cheryl will defend me to the death and Eileen needs to keep her on side for the up and coming fracas. "His name is Brutus, Mike", Cheryl says, as she draws her eyes slowly away for her mother. Mike leans over to pat my head. Just before his hand lands, he thinks better of it and pulls back. He's sensitive. He knew I had another round in the chamber and I was about to let it rip. I like him even more. I'll hold on to it, just in case I need it for the journey home. A little gift for torn face. No reason to overdo it right now. You see, Mike's not the only one with the power of restraint. Woof Woof. Mike carries on where he left off, and asks Eileen and Cheryl if they have any questions or concerns about the task ahead. Eileen's quick to get her oar in the water. "YES....I do, as it goes Michael." Mike takes a soft inhale and responds in a gentle tone, "Please Eileen, I prefer to be called Mike. If you would be so kind." Eileen lifts her lip on the left this time and says, "we'll I suppose so. Can't-do any harm." She stared at Mike throughout every word, but he wasn't fazed. Let the games begin, I say. Eileen's quick out of the blocks and asks Mike to explain, exactly, what they are here for. Mike thanks her for her question and with the same soft tone, he says, " Today, Kevin has agreed to make amends to his family for the damage he has caused throughout his drug use. This is part of step number eight in the twelve-step programme. The process will help Kevin to be accountable, and take responsibility for his behaviour. In doing so, we hope that the family can be reunited and move into the future more positively. Usually, the person making the amends, which is Kevin , writes down a list of the harms he has caused, then reads them out and asks for forgiveness. However, Kevin has agreed to do this verbally and he assures me that he is aware of his actions. Does that sound OK with you Eileen? And you Cheryl?" Eileen and Cheryl look at each other in the same way again. They turn back to Mike and nod in unison. Cheryl wants to give her brother a hug. In her own way, she's glad to see him. But, she doesn't want to incur the wrath of you-know-who. Mike steps in again, "Ok with you too Kevin?"

"Yes, Mike. Thanks," Kevin replies.

Mike lays down the ground rules. "So everyone. Kevin will talk first, and then Mother and Sister will have the opportunity to respond afterwards. Does that suit everyone?"

Yeses and nods all round.

"Ok Kevin. If you'd like to start."

Silence.

Kevin looks a bit funny! He's coming over all wishy-washy and looks as if he's gonna faint. Suddenly, he opens his eyes and starts talking. His voice seems deeper than usual.

"Cheryl," he says. "I'm sorry that I wasn't a better brother.

We grew up together and we were always really close. I'm sorry for abandoning you and for not taking care of our relationship. I love you. I always have."

Cheryl tries to hold it together, but she can't. She burst into tears. After the first few sobs, she lets go properly and falls forward in her chair to put her head in her hands on her knees. Kevin leans over and puts his hand on her back to comfort her. Eileen swipes it away. At the same time, she bitterly scolds Kevin and says, "You see. You've done it again. Look at the state you've got your sister in. I knew this would happen. I don't know why we bothered to come. You'll never change. Always the same. Kevin, Kevin, Kevin. It's all about fucking Kevin. C'mon Cheryl. We're leaving."

Kevin looks straight at her and responds. "Mother."

No one takes notice. They cant really hear him because Cheryl is wailing as hard as she can. So Kevin waits until she calms down a bit. Then he has another go.

"Mother," he says again.

"WHAAAT", she replies.

Cheryl feels the oncoming storm. She starts to stop crying and moves into occasional snot-sobs. Kevin stares through Eileen for a bit, and again she says, "WHAT IS IT?

He responds, "I've been thinking about the damage and hurt and I've caused over the years and how I've created trouble through my drug use and behaviour. While I've been here, I've had a chance to reflect on the past in an attempt to figure out why I behave the way I do. I've worked it out. So, here's what I have to say to you."

Silence again.

Then Kevin goes back into that wishy-washy-woozy look and comes over all trance-like. Slowly, he lifts his head and lets it go.

"Fuck You Mother.

Fuck you, because you tried to annihilate me. You tried to systematically stamp out my existence.

Fuck you Mother, because you deny what you have done to me and behave as if I deserved it. One time, I asked you why physically punished me as a child and why you don't hit your grandchildren now, especially Tilly and Jack. You didn't say it was because Natalie wouldn't allow it. Instead, all you could say was that that children are much cleverer than they used to be. So, it seems you are saying that you assaulted me for my own good. That it was to make me more intelligent. To make me see sense. And in turn, I should be grateful. Fuck you Mother. I was an amazingly intelligent and bright child. You tried to extinguish my light. You did everything in your power to snuff out my flame.

And Fuck you mother, because you always looked away when I needed you to see me. In fact you did more than just look away. You looked away and made sure that I knew about it. It wasn't as if you were distressed and upset or unwell and unable to care for me. You were on your feet. Above me. Looking down. You fucking directed your hatred straight at me, and my reactions let you know that the bolt had hit its target. You saw how I buckled under the weight of your malicious intent. Fuck you mother. I had the right to exist and flourish and you did everything you could to destroy this.

And Fuck you Mother because you're a tyrant. You abused and neglected me because you don't have the courage to take responsibility and face your own pain. I don't give a fuck what excuses you come up with. You strut about demonstrating that you're not afraid of anyone and how big and tough you are. Real big tough people don't ease their pain by preying on defenceless children when no one can see them. But I was there. And we both know what you did. When I was an adult and went to prison, you had the audacity to tell people how ashamed you were. People like you are going to prison every week nowadays. You are no different from them. You are the real criminal. Fuck you Mother for your lack of humanity.

And Fuck you Mother because I feel guilty for saying this. You made me utterly dependent on you by punishing me for trying to defend myself and punishing me for failing to defend myself. You punished me for feeling and punished me for avoiding my feelings. You took away my ability to protect myself and my ability to ask for help when I needed it. You set me up and then cast me adrift in the world where you had burned my home to the ground and smashed my compass. Fuck you mother for this cruelty. I let people piss and shit on me because of this. I was a courageous and loving boy. I knew how to fight and how to seek comfort, and you did everything in your power to cripple and disable my instincts.

And Fuck you mother for my rage; and for every needle that I stuck in my veins to help me survive it. These wounds were directed at you. They were there for you to see and witness what you have done. But they are a useless cry, because your entrenched self-pity will not allow you to consider, even for one second, that you are absolutely responsible for all of this.

Your thoughts will only be for you and how I have caused your pain. Nothing I say or do will ever change this. Fuck you mother for your narcissism. I was an innocent child who needed love, care and guidance in this fucked up world and you deprived me of these things and replaced them abject rejection and hatred. You poisoned me.

And Fuck you mother for putting me in a state of total panic, and for making me believe that this was my natural condition. You made me believe that was a fucked up human being, and that it was my fault. You manipulated and conditioned me into believing that I was worthless and you used abuse and insidious tactics to get me there. Your most harmful technique was silent scorn. I knew that I was taking the brunt of your shit and you made me feel responsible for it. It was as if all your illnesses and pains were my fault, and only I had the power to help you. And I would have. But you made sure that I knew you would never accept my help. Again, this put me in a place where my actions or inactions resulted in severe punishment; the threat of abandonment and death. Again, I had nowhere to go and no one to turn to. I had to disappear. I had to disconnect from myself to survive. Fuck you Mother for your brutality and exploitation. I was a warm, loving, caring and sensitive child. I had so much to give. You shackled and crushed my capacity for love.

And Fuck you Mother for trying to convince everyone around me that I was the problem in your life. You used my sisters and extended family to build a team around yourself to justify your cruelty and you used this strategy to isolate me forever. Even till this day, you have kept your barbed hooks in me to keep me from moving. I have stood on the outside looking in for as long as I can remember. No wonder the feelings of loneliness in me are so severe. Fuck you Mother for this sadistic behaviour. You built my desert, put me in it and left me there to die. You created my drought and barred me from the well, and you made me watch while others drank. You robbed me of my ability to be in relationship with all living things.

And Fuck you Mother for the way you used ambush, shock and violence to tear my creativity from me. You smothered my imagination in your bitter resentment whenever you caught me expressing myself. You actually set fuckin traps for me and snared me in them. I froze, and you only let me go when you witnessed the wash of shame come up in me. Then you turned away and left me feeling responsible for my pain and yours. Fuck you Mother for this torture. You made sure that I would never be able to succeed and that all my efforts to create would leave me feeling worthless and riddled with guilt and shame. Nothing I did would ever be good enough. I was an exceptionally gifted little boy. You desecrated this sacred source of abundance in me and left it to rot.

And Fuck you Mother for letting my father hurt me when I was a child. And fuck him to too. But Fuck you before him, because you were supposed to die for me. You should have put your life on the line for me. That's what a mother does. The only reason he ever hurt or neglected me in any way is because you let him. Fuck you mother for not bringing healthy men into my life to show me how to be male. This has left me with a fucked up idea of what a man is supposed to be and do.

And Fuck you Mother for ridiculing me about my body when I was a small child. . You were supposed to make me realise that my body was absolutely original. That there was not, and never would be another one just like it. That it was my special gift; that it was my precious thing. Fuck you for not teaching me how to look after it and treat it with loving kindness and respect at all times. I had the right to protect my body and never let anyone touch unless I allowed them too. Fuck you mother for polluting me with your shame. This has left me hating my physical appearance and believing that my body is a hostile and ugly place to live.

Fuck you for all of this Mother. And fuck you because your legacy lives on in me now. And fuck you for all the pain and hard work that I need to do, to get rid of the parts of me that have no right to be there. And fuck you for all the tired and pathetic excuses you come up with to avoid the truth. And fuck you for sitting in your self-pity now, and telling everyone around you how bad things are for you.

But more than anything else Mother. Fuck you for being you.

Mike has asked me to consider values, such as forgiveness and acceptance. Fuck those things as well. I cannot forgive the unforgivable, and I cannot accept the unacceptable. No one can. And what you did was, unforgivable and unacceptable.

But before I finish Mother. Know this. You failed to annihilate me or snuff out my flame, and you failed to leave me isolated forever. You failed to rob my creativity and crush my capacity for love. You failed to destroy my ability to be in relationship with all living things and you failed to stamp out my right to exist and flourish. More than anything else, you failed to cripple and disable my capacity to be human. What you don't know, is that something in me helped me to survive you, and you will never be able to touch it. So Fuck you Mother."

Eileen looked blank. The only thing she had to say was, "NO KEVIN.   FUCK YOU!"

Printed in Poland
by Amazon Fulfillment
Poland Sp. z o.o., Wrocław